A Note from Theo

When I was younger my nickname was TJ and
like the character in my book I didn't begin
playing football seriously until I was ten years
old. Just seven years later when I was 17 I was
called up for the England squad for the World
Cup in Germany!

Me and my friends were really lucky at school.
We had a PE teacher who always helped us and
was always on our side. He was a bit like Mr
Wood in the story. There are bits of me in the
story too . . .

Keep playing and practising!

Who knows what might happen to you – maybe
you will get the chance to play for your country
some day!

14

Theo Walcott

Access your secret bonus content!

Every Theo Walcott T.J. book has SECRET

bonus content online! It could be a cool

download, football tips, a secret story . . .

or something even more exciting!

Check it out at:

www.theowalcottbooks.co.uk/hattrick

Also available by Theo Walcott:

T.J. AND THE PENALTY

Coming soon:

T.J. AND THE CUP RUN

T.J. AND THE WINNING GOAL

THEO WALCOTT

WITH PAUL MAY

T.J. AND THE HAT-TRICK

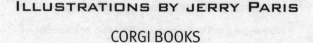

ILLUSTRATIONS BY JERRY PARIS

CORGI BOOKS

T.J. AND THE HAT-TRICK
A CORGI BOOK 978 0 552 56245 4

Published in Great Britain by Corgi Books,
an imprint of Random House Children's Books
A Random House Group Company

This edition published 2010

3 5 7 9 10 8 6 4 2

The Random House Group Limited supports the Forest Stewardship Council (FSC), the
leading international forest certification organization. All our titles that are printed on
Greenpeace-approved FSC-certified paper carry the FSC logo. Our paper procurement
policy can be found at www.rbooks.co.uk/environment.

Mixed Sources
Product group from well-managed
forests and other controlled sources
www.fsc.org Cert no. TF-COC-2139
© 1996 Forest Stewardship Council

FSC

Set in 14/22pt Meta Normal

Corgi Books are published by Random House Children's Books,
61–63 Uxbridge Road, London W5 5SA

www.**kids**at**random**house.co.uk
www.**rbooks**.co.uk

Addresses for companies within The Random House Group Limited can be found at:
www.randomhouse.co.uk/offices.htm

THE RANDOM HOUSE GROUP Limited Reg. No. 954009

A CIP catalogue record for this book is available from the British Library.

Printed and bound in Great Britain by CPI Bookmarque, Croydon, CR0 4TD

Squad Sheet

TJ: A skilful forward with an outstanding turn of speed. He has an incredibly powerful shot, and he's good in the air too.

Tulsi: A strong, powerful striker. When she has the ball at her feet all she thinks about is scoring!

Rodrigo: He's from Portugal and he doesn't speak much English, but he's a wizard with a football in midfield or defence.

Rafi: A midfielder who never stops running and tackling. His mazy runs are legendary and he always brings a ball to school!

Tommy: When he's not skateboarding he's a fearsome tackler in Parkview's defence.

Jamie: A big, strong defender. It's almost impossible to get past him, but when he clears the ball it could go anywhere.

Danny: He's not popular, but he's a terrific defender and Parkview can't do without him.

Ariyan: He can play anywhere and do a good job for the team. A really useful squad member.

Cameron: He plays in midfield or defence. Always works hard and almost never gives the ball away.

Rob: The team statistician. He dreams about being a footballer, but he's too nervous to join in training.

FOR MY MUM AND DAD

A special thanks to Caroline McAteer and
Pippa Hancock from The Sports PR Company
and Jonathan Harris from Luxton Harris Ltd

CHAPTER 1

'What do you think?' asked Tulsi. 'Shall we ask him to play?'

'He'll get those shiny shoes dirty,' said Jamie.

For a moment they both looked at the new boy, TJ, who was standing nervously on the edge of the playground. Suddenly Tulsi grinned. 'Hey, you!' she yelled. 'D'you want a game?'

Before he could reply, she put the ball down and hit a beautiful, curving pass towards him. It curled behind the kids from Class 2 and thudded into TJ's chest.

1

'What the . . . ?' TJ looked down at the muddy mark on his clean white shirt, and then he laughed. He bent down and picked up the ball. 'Here,' he said, walking towards them. 'That was amazing! Can you do it again?'

'Don't encourage her,' said Jamie. 'She already thinks she's a superstar.'

'I don't *think*,' Tulsi said. 'I *know*. I play for a proper team,' she told TJ. 'Canby Road Girls. We won the league last season and I scored eleven goals. I'm Tulsi and this is Jamie.'

Jamie was a giant, with spiky, hedgehog hair and the widest smile TJ had ever seen. Another boy ran past and knocked the

ball out of Tulsi's hands onto the ground.
He dribbled away, weaving in and out of
the little kids. 'That's Rafi,' Tulsi laughed.
'It's his ball. He doesn't like standing still.'

'Do you like football?' Jamie asked TJ.

'Well, yeah. But at my last school we just
played rounders.'

'That's crazy,' said Tulsi. 'What kind of
rubbish school wouldn't let you play footie?'

'It wasn't a rubbish school,' TJ said hotly,
but Jamie interrupted.

'Don't listen to her,' he said. 'We can't
play football here either, only on the playground or in the park. And we don't even
play rounders. All the teachers hate PE.'

'And Mr Burrows dug up the playing field
last year,' Tulsi said gloomily. 'He said it
was going to be a wildlife reserve but then
he got ill and no one looked after it. The
pond leaked and the trees all died.' She
pointed at a patch of brown grass with a

big hole in the middle of it.

'You must have somewhere to do games and stuff,' said TJ.

'We were going to use the park. It's only down the road. It was all arranged and then something happened and we couldn't. I don't know why.'

'Come on,' said Jamie when the bell went. 'I bet you're in our class. It's through here.'

'I'm not sure,' TJ said. 'I came with my mum and dad yesterday and Mr Burrows said I was in Mr Wood's class.'

'That's the one,' Jamie told him. 'Mr Wood is new too. *We* haven't met him yet either.'

'We're always having new teachers,' Rafi said, as he dribbled his ball along the crowded corridor, bouncing it off the walls. 'None of them can stand it for long.'

'He'll take one look and then go home again,' Tulsi said. She pushed the classroom door open. Everyone was yelling. Two boys were throwing a bag backwards and forwards and another boy was buzzing around them like a small, angry bee, trying to grab it back.

'Hey, Danny!' yelled Jamie, striding forward and catching the bag. 'Leave Rob alone.'

Danny made another grab for the bag, and he and Jamie fell to the floor in a heap, knocking over a couple of chairs. TJ stepped backwards just as Rafi was trying to balance his football on his nose and the ball went bouncing off across the classroom. Suddenly everything went quiet. TJ looked round and saw a tall man in a suit standing in the middle of the classroom. He looked down at the bouncing ball.

'I suppose this is how you got rid of all those teachers last year,' the man said finally. 'Well, you won't get rid of me so easily. Who does this ball belong to?'

'Me,' said Rafi. 'I'm Rafi.'

'I'm pleased to meet you, Rafi. I'm Mr Wood, and your ball control is terrible. I'll look after this until it improves, I think.'

Mr Wood put his foot on the ball, and then suddenly it was in his hands. It was like magic.

'But, sir,' said Rafi. 'It's the only ball we've got.'

'Tough. Like I say, you should learn to control it. Now, if these two clowns who are rolling around on the floor will get up, maybe we can get on with some work.'

CHAPTER 2

'I hate him,' said Tulsi in the playground after lunch.

'He's the scariest teacher we've ever had,' Jamie said.

'He's mean,' grumbled Rafi. 'He stole my ball.'

'Yeah, but he's right, isn't he?' Tulsi said. 'You can't control it. And now we've got nothing to play with.'

'Maybe you should try bringing your own ball sometimes,' Rafi replied angrily.

'Stop arguing, you two,' said Jamie. 'We can play with this fir cone. Me and TJ against you and Rafi. Here, TJ.'

The fir cone bobbled over the tarmac. TJ kicked it, and it went spinning off across the playground. They all ran after it, dodging between the other kids. TJ reached the wall where the cone had stopped. He turned round, laughing. The others were still plodding towards him. The small boy, Rob, was following behind them with a notebook in his hand.

'How did you get to be that quick?' asked Tulsi.

'Dunno,' said TJ. 'Look out. Here comes Mr Wood.'

'Stand on that cone,' Jamie hissed. 'We're not supposed to play with them.'

TJ put his foot on the cone as Mr Wood approached. 'So, what are you lot up to now?' he asked.

'Nothing, Mr Wood,' Rafi said.

The teacher looked at them for a moment or two, then he brought out Rafi's football from behind his back. 'Well,' he said, 'I wouldn't want you to get into trouble for playing with fir cones, and your ball control isn't going to improve if you don't practise, is it?'

They all shook their heads. Mr Wood looked around at the crowded playground and the brown grass with the dead trees.

'There's not much room to play, is there?' he said. 'Where do you do PE?'

'We don't,' Tulsi said. 'Not since Mr Potter left, and even then it was rubb—' She stopped, embarrassed.

'I get the picture,' Mr Wood said. He looked at the grass again and shook his head. 'Listen, I'll tell the Midday Supervisors to keep the little ones off this part of the playground. You could use that bit of wall as a goal.'

They were all speechless. Mr Wood turned and walked away to speak to Janice, the head dinner lady. Halfway there, he paused. 'No more football in the classroom, OK?' he said. They all nodded.

'I don't believe it,' Rafi said.

'We've *never* had our own bit of the playground,' said Tulsi. 'Who's going in goal? Headers and volleys, OK?'

'Me,' said TJ. 'I've always wanted to be a goalie.'

Tulsi and Rafi were attackers and Jamie was the defender. Tulsi lifted the ball into the air with one foot and tried to knock it over Jamie's head to where Rafi was waiting. Jamie jumped and the ball cannoned off the back of his head straight at TJ's goal. TJ moved quickly to one side and plucked the ball out of the air.

'Hey!' said Tulsi. 'That was good. Maybe you really *are* a goalkeeper.'

TJ was enjoying himself. He stopped almost everything they headed or volleyed at him. Then Tulsi missed with a volley.

'Go on, TJ,' she said. 'My turn in goal.'

TJ glanced over at Rob, who was writing something in his notebook. TJ wondered what it was.

'Have you played this game before?' Jamie asked him.

TJ shook his head. 'Not exactly like this.'

'It's dead simple. It's me and you attacking. We're only allowed to score with headers or volleys. If you miss, like Tulsi just did, then you go in goal. Or if you score five. That's the way we play, anyway. Here, I'll cross it for you.'

'I hate headers,' TJ began, but the ball was already flying towards him. Oh, well, he thought. I might as well try. He squeezed his eyes shut and felt a stinging thud as the ball collided with his nose. It always happened.

'Nice one,' called Jamie. 'Oh!'

TJ opened his eyes and saw the ball ballooning high over the wall and into the garden beyond. They all stood, listening.

'I don't think it broke anything,' Tulsi said at last.

Rafi looked around the playground. Janice was busy with a little girl who'd cut her knee and all the other dinner ladies were laughing together. No one was watching. 'We can get it if we're quick,' Rafi said.

'Jamie should go,' said Tulsi. 'It was a terrible cross.'

TJ looked at the wall. He could climb it easily. 'I headed it,' he said. 'I'll go.' And before they could argue he had pulled himself up onto the top of the wall and dropped into the garden below.

CHAPTER 3

TJ had landed in the middle of some very prickly bushes. His heart was beating fast. What if there was a fierce dog? What if there was someone actually in the garden?

He peered out from between the bushes. He could see a narrow strip of grass, and flower beds, and some garden chairs. He could see the windows staring down at him like eyes, but he couldn't see the football. The shouts from the playground on the other side of the wall seemed a long way away. Then he heard Tulsi's voice as her head popped over the wall.

'It's down there,' she hissed, pointing. 'By that chair. Quick!'

TJ ran out from the bushes, dashed across the grass and picked up the ball. When he turned back, Tulsi's face had gone. He ran to the foot of the wall, chucked the ball over, and began to climb. 'It was easy,' he said, as he reached the top. 'I—'

He stopped. There wasn't a sound from the playground. He looked down and saw Janice and the other dinner ladies, all standing there looking up at him.

But that wasn't all. A woman teacher with a long skirt and a little black jacket was walking across the playground towards them. She had short grey hair and enormous glasses that made her eyes look huge. 'You, boy!' she yelled at TJ, waving her hand at him. 'Get down from there at once.'

Danny was walking by her side. 'I told you, Mrs Logan,' he said. 'Mr Wood confiscated that ball this morning. I bet they nicked it from the classroom.'

'No, we didn't,' Tulsi said. 'Mr Wood brought us the ball himself. And he said we could play here.'

'Be quiet, Tulsi,' Mrs Logan snapped. 'Give me that football, Rafi, and go and stand by the wall. And the rest of you too. No, not you,' she said to TJ. 'You can have a word with Mr Burrows. I haven't met you before, have I?'

'No, miss,' TJ said. 'I'm new. This is my first day.'

'Wait,' called Mr Wood, hurrying across the playground. 'Is there a problem, Mrs Logan?'

'I should jolly well think there is, Mr Wood. The children in your class have been causing havoc with this football, which they took from your classroom without permission.'

'I think there's been a misunderstanding,' Mr Wood said with a smile. 'I gave them the ball. And I asked these lovely ladies to clear a space for them to practise in. Isn't that right, ladies?'

Janice laughed. 'It's true, Mrs Logan. Rafi and his friends were playing nicely too.'

Mrs Logan started to go red. She gave Danny a very nasty look. 'Well,' she said finally. 'That doesn't alter the fact that this boy was caught red-handed climbing over the wall. He's in serious trouble.'

'Well, it is his first day,' Mr Wood said. 'Do you mind if I deal with him, Mrs Logan?'

'Fine,' Mrs Logan said, after a long pause. 'But I shall be keeping an eye on you, young man.'

'Did you cause any damage?' Mr Wood asked TJ as Mrs Logan walked away with her nose in the air.

'No, Mr Wood.'

'Well, even so, it wasn't a sensible thing to do. Don't do it again.'

'I won't. Sorry, Mr Wood.'

TJ *tried* to look sorry, but it was hard, because he could see that there was a glint in Mr Wood's eye as he gazed after Mrs Logan.

'What you kids need is a football pitch,' he said, looking at the brown grass.

'It's a shame,' said Janice, the dinner lady. 'There's nothing for the kids to do at break times. You can't blame them if they get a bit wild sometimes.'

'Well, why don't we give them something to play with?' said Mr Wood. 'We could get some more balls out. And skipping ropes. How about that?'

'You'll be lucky,' Janice said. 'The PE cupboard is locked and most of the stuff in there is about a million years old.'

'I'll have a word with Mr Burrows. And

meanwhile, TJ, no more rock-climbing, OK?'
TJ nodded.

'The rest of you, you'd better practise,'
Mr Wood said, chucking the ball to Rafi.
'You're going to need it!'

'What did he mean?' asked Rafi.

'No idea,' Tulsi said. 'Come on, TJ. Perhaps it'll be safer if you go back in goal.'

CHAPTER 4

'We go to the park after school, most nights,'
Jamie said at the end of the day. 'Are you
coming, TJ?'

'Maybe tomorrow,' TJ said. 'I'd better not
be late home.'

He watched Jamie, Rafi and Tulsi run off
down the street, Rafi dribbling his football.
TJ wondered if he took it to bed with him at
night. Then he heard a shout and saw Rob
running towards him. Danny and his friend
Carl were chasing him. They stopped and
walked off when they saw TJ. 'Yeah, go on, you
cowards,' Rob yelled after them. 'Run away!'

'Hey,' said TJ. 'There's no need to wind them up.'

'Well, they *are* cowards,' Rob said. 'They only pick on me 'cause I'm small.'

'Where do you live?' TJ asked.

'Churchill Road.'

'That's on the way to my house, I think. Come on. We can go together.'

They walked a short way. 'Hey, Rob,' asked TJ. 'What do you write in that note-book of yours?'

'You'll laugh,' Rob said.

'No, I won't.'

'OK, then,' said Rob after a moment. He stopped and took the notebook out of his bag. 'I collect stats,' he said. 'Like, this is Wanderers v Arsenal last weekend, see? Goal attempts, passes completed, corners, goal kicks. It's not as accurate as I'd like it to be,' he went on very seriously, 'because you can't see everything on the TV. The clubs use computers and video cameras.'

Arsenal		Wanderers
0		2
18	shots	16
6	shots on target	6
281	Passes	295
16	Crosses	13
6	offsides	1

Wanderers

Passes: ||||| ||||| ||||| ||||| ||||| ||||| ||||| ||||| ||||| ||||| ||||| ||||| ||||| ||||| ||||| ||||| ||||| ||||| ||||| ||||| ||||| ||||| ||||| ||||| ||||| ||||| ||||| ||||| ||||| ||||| ||||| ||||| ||||| ||||| ||||| ||||| ||||| ||||| ||||| ||||| ||||| ||||| ||||| || 227

Intercepted passes: ||||| ||||| ||||| ||||| ||||| ||||| ||||| ||||| ||||| ||||| ||||| ||||| ||||| ||||| ||||| ||||| ||| 89

TJ stared at the pages of numbers and the clever little diagrams Rob had drawn. 'These are amazing,' he said. 'But what were you doing at lunch time?'

'I'll show you. Look, this is you in goal. Twelve saves to your right. Five to your left. Not bad.'

'Thanks,' said TJ.

'That header was rubbish though,' Rob continued.

TJ laughed. 'I hate heading the ball. It always smacks me in the face.'

'That's because you shut your eyes. You need to practise.'

'So how come you don't play if you know all this stuff?'

'I'm no good. I'm too small and my glasses might fall off and get broken. This is my street. Bye.'

'See you tomorrow,' TJ called after him. Rob was the oddest boy he had ever met, but he couldn't help liking him. He jogged the rest of the way home, squeezed past the piles of boxes in the hallway and found his mum in the kitchen. They had only moved in three days before.

'How was your first day?' she asked. 'There's no food in the house, I'm afraid. Dad's picking up a takeaway on his way home. He won't be long. You can start unpacking the stuff in your room.'

'Actually, Mum,' TJ said, 'I was wondering if you knew which box had the football in it?'

'Football?'

'They're all crazy about it at school. I want to practise. And I need to learn to do headers properly.'

'Try the box with the garden stuff. And change out of those clothes. The washing machine won't be working till tomorrow.'

TJ found the ball and took it into the back garden. There was a brick wall at the end. He threw the ball against it and headed it back again, trying to keep his eyes wide open, like Rob had told him. It wasn't as hard as he'd expected, although he still wasn't sure he'd want to head one of Jamie's crosses.

He headed the ball a few more times, just to make sure he'd got the hang of it. Then he started kicking it, trying to keep it bouncing. That was easy, so he began to use both feet, left then right. He was so absorbed that he didn't notice his big brother, Joey, come into the garden. He jumped when Joey spoke.

'Hey, pretty impressive, little brother. I didn't know you could do stuff like that.'

'Me neither,' said TJ. 'I played football at school today. I went in goal. I saved' – he paused, trying to remember Rob's stats – 'seventeen shots. I've decided to be a goalie. It's cool.'

Joey laughed. 'Or you could be a juggler, doing stuff like that. Come on, Dad's home. It's time to eat.'

They went inside and found their dad dishing out curry. 'Hey, TJ,' he said. 'How did it go?'

'It was great,' said TJ. 'I made friends. And my teacher is brilliant.'

'You don't have to pretend, TJ. You know we wouldn't have sent you to Parkview if

Hillside had had room.'

'Honest, Dad, I liked it.'

'Well, you make sure you tell us if you have any problems, OK? If there's trouble I'll be in there like a shot.'

'It's fine, Dad, really.' TJ suddenly remembered how close he'd been to trouble that day and felt a little shaky.

'TJ's started playing football,' Joey said, changing the subject. TJ looked at him gratefully.

'Yeah?' said his dad. 'Excellent! We'll go out back after we've eaten and I'll show you a few moves.'

Joey groaned and raised his eyebrows at TJ. They had both seen their dad's moves before. 'I don't think so,' Mrs Wilson said. 'You have to finish Lou's bedroom, remember?' Lou was TJ's sister. She was fifteen. 'And when you've done that, there's all these boxes.'

*

TJ unpacked boxes for a while after they'd
eaten, but when they'd all had enough,
and were sitting on the sofa watching TV,
TJ slipped out into the back garden again.
He'd remembered that first pass that Tulsi
had hit to him on the playground that
morning. How had she made it curve like
that? She'd somehow used the outside of
her foot to make the ball spin and move in
the air. He kicked hard, trying to just catch
the edge of the ball, but it spun away
uselessly into the flower bed and TJ found
himself lying flat on his back. He stood up
and tried again. This time the ball flew
straight at the wall, bounced off and
smacked him in the face.

'Third time lucky,' he told himself,
wiping the mud from his cheek. He placed
the ball carefully and worked out exactly
where he wanted to strike it. This time, his

foot connected perfectly. He watched the ball swerve through the air, and trapped it neatly as it returned to his feet. That was good, he thought, but it was just one time. He needed to be able to do it *every* time.

He began to practise.

CHAPTER 5

'Well, now,' said Mr Wood the following morning. 'I've noticed that some of you are very keen on football. I think it's about time this school had a football team, don't you?'

Tulsi put her hand up. 'But Mr Wood, we haven't got anywhere to play. How can we have a team?'

'We're going to have to think about that,' Mr Wood said. 'I've got a few ideas, but meanwhile I want to start training. We'll have to use the playground for now. It's not ideal, and we won't be able to practise tackling, but at least we can make a start.

We'll have our first training session tomorrow night after school. Sign up here if you're coming. And there's a letter for you to take home.'

He pinned a piece of paper to the wall.

SIGN UP HERE FOR
FOOTBALL TRAINING:

There was a knock on the door and a teacher TJ hadn't seen before came in. She was young, with straight, dark hair and a lopsided smile. 'Hello, Mr Wood,' she said. 'I've come for Rob and Shahnaz.'

'Who's that,' TJ whispered to Jamie, as Rob and one of the girls stood up to leave.

'Miss Berry. She does stuff with kids who need extra help. You know, reading and stuff.'

'But Rob's clever. I saw—'

'Be quiet over there. We're ready to begin.'

TJ bent over his book. He remembered what his dad had said. He needed to keep out of trouble.

At the end of the day there were only five names on Mr Wood's list. Tulsi, Jamie, Rafi, TJ and Danny. 'Why did Danny have to go and put his name down?' asked Jamie disgustedly.

'It's a good thing he did,' Rafi said. 'We need everyone we can get. And anyway, he might be good.'

'Good at kicking people,' replied Jamie.

'You see,' said Tulsi. 'It's pointless. I knew it would be. If you want to play football, you should join a team like mine.'

'There must be other people,' TJ said. 'Hey, Tommy,' he called to the red-headed boy who was just leaving. 'Don't you want to come?'

'Nah,' said Tommy. 'Concrete's for skateboards, not footie. And you won't have much of a team with five people. Especially if one of them's Danny.'

'What about you, Rodrigo?' TJ asked. 'You're from Portugal. Portugal's good at football.' He didn't expect Rodrigo to reply, because Rodrigo hadn't spoken a word all day. TJ felt sorry for him. It was bad enough being new. It must be a whole lot worse if you couldn't even speak English.

But Rodrigo's face broke into a smile when TJ said 'football'. 'Football,' Rodrigo repeated. 'Football good.'

'Hey,' said Jamie. 'You *can* talk, Rodrigo. Great!'

Mr Wood came back into the classroom.

'Hmmm,' he said, looking at the list.

'Rodrigo might come,' Rafi said, 'only I don't think he understands.'

Mr Wood waved a piece of paper. 'I

know,' he said. 'That's why I've just had this translated into Portuguese. Here, Rodrigo, give this to your mum.' He showed Rodrigo what he had written, and Rodrigo nodded happily. 'Now, you lot. Get off home. And make sure you tell people to come to training.'

Rob was waiting for TJ outside. 'Sorry, Rob,' TJ said. 'I can't walk home with you. We're going to the park.'

TJ had asked Mum and Dad at breakfast. His dad had offered to come along to show them his moves. TJ hoped he'd been joking.

'I'll come and watch,' Rob said.

'Great,' said TJ, but Tulsi groaned.

'We don't want him hanging around,' she muttered to Jamie, but Jamie shrugged.

'I don't see why he can't come if he wants,' he said. 'It's a free country.'

'I'll go in goal,' TJ said, when they reached the park. They piled up their bags for one goalpost. The other was a bench. Rob sat down close to TJ and pulled out his notebook.

'We'll play three and in, OK?' said Rafi. 'All against all.' He put the ball down and hit the ball at TJ, who instinctively volleyed it away over the heads of the others, just as he'd been practising in the back garden. They all raced off into the distance.

'Pretty good,' Rob said, making a note in his book. 'Nice technique. You might need to get your knee over the ball a little more if you were shooting, of course, but excellent for a clearance.'

Rafi had reached the ball first and he was now dribbling it off among some trees near the park entrance. Jamie had given up chasing him, but Tulsi was running after him and yelling that the ball was out of play.

'Why don't you come to training?' TJ asked Rob, but Rob shook his head.

'I'm going to do the stats,' he said. 'If Mr Wood manages to get a team together, you'll need someone to analyse the performances. I might even write the match reports.'

TJ was about to argue when two boys and a girl rode up on bikes and stopped in front of them. One of the boys was very short, about Rob's height, but much wider, with braided hair.

'Do you want a game?' the boy asked, as Tulsi and Jamie got back, both of them out of breath.

'OK,' Tulsi said, 'but there's only three of you.'

'Doesn't matter,' said the girl. 'We'll have a rush goalie. We'll thrash you anyway.'

TJ couldn't help noticing that they all had expensive trainers on their feet. 'Where are they from?' he asked.

'Hillside,' said Jamie. 'They really think they're something, don't they?

TJ nodded. He'd been to visit Hillside with his mum and dad, before they'd found out that he couldn't go there. It was on the edge of town, with big grassy fields and modern buildings. He looked at his new friends and realized that he was glad that he had gone to Parkview instead.

'Look out,' said Rob. 'Here they come.'

CHAPTER 6

It didn't take TJ long to learn the names of
the kids from Hillside. The little round one
was Kelvin, the tall skinny boy was Slim, and
the girl was Krissy. They shouted to each
other all the time. Krissy passed to Slim, and
Tulsi and Rafi both ran to tackle him.

'No!' Tulsi yelled at Rafi. 'Get over there
and mark the other one.'

It was far too late. Slim controlled the ball
neatly and passed to Kelvin. He simply
clipped it to one side of Jamie where Krissy
was running at top speed. She took the ball
in her stride, touched it once, and blasted it

past TJ, who didn't even have time to move.

'Goal!' said Rob, scribbling fast in his notebook. 'Right-footed drive to the top right-hand corner. Assist from Kelvin. Bad luck, TJ. You had no chance.'

TJ rolled the ball to Jamie. 'Give it here,' said Rafi, running up to him. 'Come on, Jamie.'

'Get rid of it!' yelled Tulsi, who had raced to the other end and was waiting by the Hillside goal. 'Clear it, Jamie!'

Jamie panicked as Kelvin raced towards him. He whacked the ball as hard as he could and it rocketed away towards the gate. Then it hit a lamppost and rebounded to land at Krissy's feet. She passed to Slim, who passed to Kelvin, who shot the ball past TJ.

Tulsi, Rafi and Jamie were all shouting at each other now.

'You can't just stand by their goal!' Jamie yelled at Tulsi. 'How can anyone pass to you all the way over there?'

'Someone with a bit of talent, maybe,' said Tulsi. 'Someone who looked where he was kicking it.'

'We're off now,' said Krissy. 'Thanks for the game.'

TJ watched them skid out of the gate. 'It looks like we need quite a lot of training,' he said to Rob, who was still writing.

'Hillside do have one of the most successful school teams in the area,' Rob said, without looking up. The others were busy having an argument. 'They were runners-up in the league last year. Krissy Barton scored eighteen goals.'

'How do you know all this stuff?' TJ asked.

'The results are all on the Internet,' Rob said. 'It's easy. Only it seemed a bit pointless when we didn't have a team. But now it could be very useful.'

Hillside League Stats

Team	P	W	D	L	F	A	W	D	L	F	A	GD	Pts.
St.Josephs	12	5	1	0	17	3	5	0	1	17	6	+25	31
Hillside	12	5	1	0	15	6	4	2	0	10	6	+13	30
Swinburne	12	3	1	2	13	10	3	2	1	11	6	+8	21
St.Martins	12	2	2	2	11	7	1	2	3	6	10	0	13
Oaktree	12	2	2	2	9	8	0	1	5	5	16	-10	8
Guildhall	12	1	2	3	7	10	0	2	4	6	11	-8	7
Bedford	12	2	0	4	7	15	0	0	6	4	24	-28	6

Key— P: played W: win D: draw L: lost F: for A: against
GD: goal difference Pts: points

'Not if we don't find some more players,'
TJ said. 'And not if the ones we've got don't
stop fighting.'

When TJ got home he handed the letter to
his mum. 'Training tomorrow night,' he said.
'We might be getting a school team.'

'Cool,' said Joey. 'Can we come and
watch?'

'We haven't got many players yet. It might
be rubbish.'

'I'll try and make it myself,' Mr Wilson
said. 'It sounds like you're going to need
some supporters.'

After lunch the next day, Mr Wood asked
Tulsi and TJ to come to the classroom.

'I might need some help,' he said, holding
up a silver key. 'Mr Burrows has given me
the key to the PE store, so we can fetch out
some equipment for training tonight, and we
can see what we can find to make break

times more interesting. First problem. Where is it?'

'Easy,' said Tulsi. 'It's at the end of that corridor there. Next to Mr Coggins' room.'

They looked down the dimly lit corridor. At the end, a single fluorescent light was flickering. Mr Wood led the way, but as he reached out to put the key in the door a tall figure in a brown coat emerged from the caretaker's room, making them all jump.

'What do you want then?' Mr Coggins demanded.

So far TJ had only glimpsed the caretaker in the distance, sweeping up leaves in the car park. Below his shiny bald head he had an enormous red nose and bulging, red-rimmed eyes.

'PE equipment,' Mr Wood said cheerfully, and Mr Coggins gave a hollow laugh that turned into a long, wheezing cough.

'Just you be careful how you open that

door,' he warned them. 'I'm not responsible if you hurt yourselves, all right?'

Mr Wood turned the key and pushed at the door. 'There seems to be something in the way,' he grunted, pushing harder. Behind them, the caretaker laughed again. 'Come on, you two. Give me a hand.'

They all shoved together and suddenly the door burst open. Broken hoops, flat footballs and leaking beanbags cascaded onto the floor. Mr Wood reached round the corner and flicked a switch. Inside the little room they saw a mountain of old wire baskets and broken equipment.

'Very dangerous,' said Mr Coggins. 'I wouldn't go in there if I were you.'

'We're not going in,' Mr Wood said. 'We're going to take it all out. Tulsi, TJ, go and fetch your friends. We'll put it all in the corridor and sort it into things we can use and things that Mr Coggins can chuck in the skip. OK, Mr Coggins?'

Mr Coggins stared at Mr Wood for a moment. 'Fill my skip with all this rubbish?' he said finally. 'You can't do that! And I'm not having my corridor filled up neither. We'll see what the boss has to say about this. Don't you touch a thing till I get back.'

CHAPTER 7

'Quick,' said Tulsi to the others on the playground. 'You have to come. There's going to be an enormous row.'

They rushed back through the school and found Mr Wood, Mr Coggins, Mr Burrows and Mrs Logan all standing in the narrow entrance to the corridor. 'I need PE equipment,' Mr Wood was saying. 'We can't train without it, and if we don't train we can't have a team. Most of this stuff should have been thrown away a long time ago. Look at it!'

'What's all this about football training?'

Mr Burrows asked, looking worried. His suit was old and crumpled, and it looked as if he'd spilt half of his breakfast on his tie. 'Football's always causing trouble around here. Broken windows. Neighbours complaining.'

'Exactly,' Mrs Logan sniffed. 'Why only yesterday I had to talk to a boy who—'

'I thought perhaps if I taught the children some skills then they wouldn't cause trouble,' Mr Wood interrupted, to TJ's relief. 'And if we gave them something to play with on the playground, maybe break times would be a little calmer.'

Mrs Logan turned suddenly and saw the children waiting. 'You children, outside please. Right now.'

They walked a few steps and saw their classroom door standing open. Jamie pointed, and they all slipped inside.

They could still hear the teachers quite clearly.

'I'm impressed by your enthusiasm, Mr Wood,' Mr Burrows was saying. 'I just hope you won't be too disappointed. You'll be very lucky if anyone at all comes to your football training. And please, try not to upset the neighbours.'

'What about my corridor?' demanded Mr Coggins. 'What about my skip with all this rubbish?'

'That's what your skip is for, Mr Coggins,' Mrs Logan said. 'I shall come and watch this football training,' she told Mr Wood. 'Just to make sure that everything is done properly.'

As soon the teachers had left, TJ and his friends went quickly out onto the playground, where Mr Wood found them a few minutes later.

'All sorted,' he said. 'Mr Coggins is finding

us a trolley. Come on, you lot.'

They passed out the things that Mr Wood excavated from the storeroom to Tulsi, who heaped most of them on the trolley as Mr Wood called out 'Rubbish!' over and over again. The room was nearly empty when Mr Wood said, 'At last!' and held up a blue-and-black striped football shirt for them to see.

'Inter Milan,' said Rob. 'It's a pity about the holes.'

It was true. All the shirts that Mr Wood pulled out of a big cardboard box were full of holes. 'Mice, I think,' he said gloomily.

'Or rats,' said Tulsi with a shudder.

'Still,' said Rob, 'there *are* some proper footballs. And some shin pads. And some cones. And even some training bibs.'

'Hey,' said Mr Wood, brightening up. 'Well spotted, Rob. Excellent. We'll get these footballs pumped up. Grab that box of skipping ropes too. And those small balls over there. We'll give them to the little ones for break times.'

'It's still no good,' Tulsi whispered to TJ as they planted seeds for their science project that afternoon. 'It's still only us going to training.'

But Rodrigo surprised them. When the bell went at the end of the afternoon, he pulled out an orange football shirt with a blue collar.

'Nice!' said Rob. 'FC Porto away kit, isn't it, Rodrigo?'

'Porto good,' grinned Rodrigo, as they made their way out onto the playground where Mr Wood was waiting. Quite a few people had gathered to watch, and TJ had the feeling that most of them had come to laugh. He saw that Mrs Logan had brought a chair outside and was sitting with a clipboard on her lap.

'She's going to give Mr Wood marks out of ten,' said Rafi.

'She'll probably knock a mark off for the hat,' Tulsi said. Mr Wood was wearing a blue baseball cap, tracksuit bottoms and a faded red T-shirt.

'OK,' the teacher said. 'Let's make a start. We'll do three laps of the field and the playground first, to warm up.'

He set off at a gentle jog and TJ was pleased to discover that he was able to keep up easily. Tulsi and Rafi followed a short way behind, but Jamie stopped after the first lap and started walking.

'Right,' said Mr Wood when they'd finished. 'Everyone take a ball.' Mr Wood, TJ noticed, wasn't out of breath at all. 'Now spread out – give yourselves a square around you about two metres each side. Just move the ball around in your square with the bottom of your foot. One foot, then the other. That's it! It's like a little dance. Keep jogging. Don't stop.'

TJ could hear Danny complaining that it was boring, but he didn't care. He was enjoying himself. He got into a rhythm, pushing the ball first one way, then the other. The rest of the world simply didn't exist.

'I said stop, TJ!' Mr Wood's voice finally got through to him, and he stood still, embarrassed. 'Nice work, everyone,' Mr Wood said. 'Just pay attention and stop when I say "stop", OK? Now then . . .'

All the exercises Mr Wood gave them to do were dead simple, but after a while TJ realized that he hardly ever let them stop moving. They dribbled in and out of rows of cones, they jumped between hoops, they passed with one foot and then the other, they controlled the ball with thighs

and chests and feet . . .

'When are you going to play a game, then?' yelled Danny's mate Carl, who'd come along to jeer. But TJ knew that they were doing some serious work. And he wasn't the only one who'd figured that out.

There was a sudden clatter of wheels and TJ saw Tommy and his mates skid to a halt on their skateboards.

'Mr Wood?' said Tommy. 'Is it OK if we join in?'

Mr Wood looked at them. 'Well, I suppose you're warmed up already,' he said. 'And we're going to have a game now, to finish off. But next time you come from the start, OK?'

Tommy and his mates grinned and parked their boards.

'These are the rules,' Mr Wood said. 'Once you have the ball under control, no one can take it off you. There are no tackles because we're playing on a hard surface here. I want to see you control the ball, pass and move. Just like the practice we've been doing. TJ, Tulsi, Jamie, Tommy and Rafi, put on these blue bibs. I'll play with Danny, Rodrigo, Cameron and Jay. We'll be the Greens.'

'I'll go in goal,' TJ said.

'You don't have to,' Tulsi told him.

'I *want* to be a goalie,' said TJ. 'Goalies are

good. They can save penalties. Everyone loves them.'

'You're crazy,' said Tulsi. 'But at least it saves us having to argue about it. Now let's show Mr Wood how absolutely brilliant we are.'

CHAPTER 8

The first thing that TJ noticed, as Mr Wood's team kicked off, was that Rodrigo knew how to play football. He was taller than the others, and gangly, but when the ball came to him he controlled it quickly. Then the trouble began. Everyone on Rodrigo's side began shouting at him.

'Hey, Rodrigo, go right!'

'Rodrigo! On the wing!'

'Watch out, Rodrigo, she's going to tackle you!'

Rodrigo was confused. TJ had to laugh. They seemed to have forgotten that Rodrigo only spoke about three words of English. Before Rodrigo had even had a chance to touch it, Tulsi whipped the ball away from his feet and blasted it at Mr Wood's goal. The ball bounced off Cameron's knee and shot away towards Tommy. Tommy chased after it but, just as he reached it, Danny stepped across and tackled him. Tommy hit the tarmac and rolled over several times.

Mr Wood blew his whistle and strode angrily towards Danny. 'I told you,' he said. 'No tackling. It's dangerous.'

'It's OK, Mr Wood,' Tommy said, pulling up his trouser leg to reveal all kinds of grazes and scabs and bruises. 'I fall off my skateboard all the time.' He grinned. 'I'm good at falling over.'

'That's not the point. Blues, it's your free kick.'

Rafi placed the ball and stepped back. Tulsi was standing in front of Mr Wood's goal, waving her arms madly and shouting for the ball. 'Go on,' Jamie said, 'boot it up to her. She'll just keep going on at you until you do.'

Rafi ran up and smacked the ball as hard as he could. It whistled past Cameron and bounced between Jay's legs. Tulsi took a couple of touches towards the goal. She did two fancy stepovers, and TJ wondered why, as there was no one to beat except the goal-keeper. She did one, final stepover and then hit her shot. She was looking around to check that everyone was admiring her skill when Mr Wood reached out a long arm and caught the ball effortlessly in one hand, like a basketball player.

Tulsi stared as he rolled it back out to Rodrigo. She had just hit her hardest shot and Mr Wood hadn't even blinked. She was still staring when Rodrigo cleared the ball and everyone else ran after it.

'It's mine,' shouted Rafi.

'No, leave it to me,' Jamie growled.

It was as if they were all playing for their own little teams, TJ thought, watching the knot of players tussling for the ball. You would never have known that Rafi and Jamie were both on his side. Then suddenly Rafi burst away with the ball and dribbled towards the goal.

'Hey!' yelled TJ. 'Where are you going? Don't—'

It was too late. Rafi shot. TJ watched the ball flying towards him and instinctively went to control it with his foot. Then he remembered he was a goalie and reached out to grab it with his hands. He was too slow. He got a fingertip to it, but it spun behind him and between the posts. While Mr Wood's team celebrated, Tulsi, Tommy and Jamie all started shouting at Rafi.

'You're all rubbish,' called a voice from outside the fence.

TJ looked over and saw a small bunch of kids from his class. 'At least we're trying,' he said, and he turned and jogged across the playground to retrieve the ball. As he picked it up he saw his brother, Joey, and his dad.

'Great,' he said. 'You're here.'

'You still like it in goal?' asked Joey.

'Yeah. Why not? And it's a way to get in the team because the others are really good.'

His dad laughed. 'Good? That lot? You'll be lucky if you ever make a team out of them. The tall kid's not bad, and that red-haired boy, but I reckon you could run rings round them. That girl's a real goal-hanger. She never moves.'

'It's only our first practice,' TJ said. 'We'll get better.' He picked up the ball and ran back to the game, leaving his family shaking their heads.

Five minutes later Mr Wood called them

all together. 'Well done, everyone,' he said. 'You've worked really hard. But if you think I'm going to tell you you're great footballers, well, I'm not.'

TJ's heart sank. He looked at the others. They all looked as fed up as he felt.

'None of you can pass the ball to save your lives,' Mr Wood continued, 'and some of you don't even seem to know which way you're supposed to shoot. But on the other hand, it seems to me that you've had a raw deal. There's been no PE for ages here, and where your football pitch should be there's a strip of grass that looks like it's been dug up by a herd of giant moles.'

They all laughed, and TJ suddenly felt a little flicker of hope.

'I can turn you into a team,' Mr Wood said. 'But only if you're all prepared to work harder than you've ever worked in your lives. I don't know yet if you'll be any good, but

you *will* be a team, and then Parkview
School will have something to be proud
of for a change. How about it? Are you up
for it?'

TJ suddenly saw the excitement glittering
in Mr Wood's blue eyes. It seemed to flicker
in the air. He could feel it, running through
him like electricity, and he realized that the
others were feeling the same thing. As he
walked home with his family. his dad said,
'You really want to do this, don't you, TJ?'

TJ nodded.

'Well, I did see one good thing out there
tonight – your Mr Wood. He seems like he
knows what he's doing.'

'I told you,' TJ said.

'Yeah, you did. And we met quite a few of
your mates' mums and dads while we were
there. Nice, friendly people. I reckon if we all
got together we could really make things
start to happen in this place. But listen,

that Mr Wood. Where's he from?'

'I don't know, Dad,' said TJ. 'Why?'

'It doesn't matter,' Mr Wilson said. 'I just had the feeling I'd seen him somewhere before, that's all.'

CHAPTER 9

It was the following Monday morning when TJ arrived in the classroom and spotted Rob writing in his notebook. 'What are you doing now?' he asked him.

'I'm finishing the stats from the training last week.'

'I didn't see you there.'

'I didn't *want* anyone to see. They'd just make fun of me if they knew.'

'I bet they wouldn't. Why don't you show them?'

Before Rob could say anything, TJ had called Rafi and Jamie over. 'Look,' he said.

'Rob's analysed our training session. It's brilliant.'

'It doesn't need analysing though, does it,' Jamie said. 'We were rubbish.'

'You have to know exactly why you were rubbish,' Rob said seriously. 'Look, Rafi, this is you.' Little black arrows darted about all over the diagram of the pitch. 'I estimate that you ran about one kilometre in five minutes.'

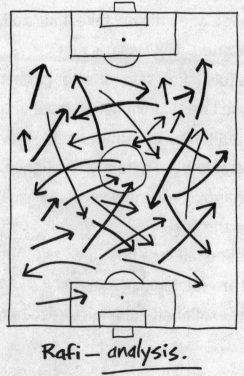

Rafi — analysis.

'That's amazing,' said Rafi, staring at the picture.

'Yeah,' said TJ. 'It's clever, isn't it? Rob does this for every game he watches.'

'Rob's a bit weird,' Rafi said. 'Everyone knows that. What I meant was, it's good that I ran all that way. I must be fast!'

'You have to run in the right direction,' said Jamie. 'Half the time you don't even know which way you are running.'

'I made one little mistake, that's all,' Rafi retorted. 'Hey, what's that?'

'It's Tulsi,' Rob said. 'It's not perfect because I was watching Rafi most of the time, but I think it's about right.' They all looked at Rob's diagram and laughed. All of the arrows were in a very small space next to the goal.

'Are you talking about me?' said Tulsi. 'What are you looking at?'

They explained Rob's picture to her.

Tulsi — analysis.

'I estimate that you ran about a hundred metres in total,' Rob said. 'Most strikers in the Premier League run about twelve kilometres in a match.'

'We're not in the Premier League, Rob,' Tulsi said angrily. 'And I don't need to run if people pass the ball to me properly, do I?

Who said you could spy on us anyway?'

'What's all this?' None of them had noticed Mr Wood entering the classroom. Now he was looking over Tulsi's shoulder at Rob's book. 'It looks like Prozone. Did you do this, Rob?' Rob shut the book quickly. 'Clear off, the rest of you,' Mr Wood said, sitting down beside him. 'Get your work out and get on with it. And no talking.'

TJ had already figured out that theirs was the only classroom in the whole school where people worked in silence. In fact, he had sometimes had the feeling that it might be the only classroom in the school where anyone worked at all. He had walked past the Reception classroom one morning and seen the teacher knitting while the little kids did exactly as they liked. The noise from the rest of the school echoed along the corridors now, as Mr Wood spoke quietly to Rob. After a few moments, TJ was amazed to see Rob

open his book and show something to Mr
Wood. Then Mr Wood said something and
Rob's face cracked into a smile.

'But Rob never smiles,' hissed Jamie to TJ.

'Quiet over there,' snapped Mr Wood.

When he'd finished talking to Rob, Mr
Wood went to the front of the class. 'I've
been busy this weekend,' he said. 'I had a
meeting with the PE teacher over at Hillside
School. She seems to think they've got a
decent football team. Perhaps you'd like to
tell everyone about them, Rob.'

'What does *he* know?' Danny muttered.

Mr Wood fixed him with a look that made
him go bright red, and then pale. It was a
look that TJ thought would make a good
secret weapon. 'Go ahead, Rob,' said
Mr Wood.

'They were . . . they . . .' Rob stopped.
His voice sounded trembly and uncertain.

'Shall I read it for you?' Mr Wood offered.

'Or one of your friends?'

Rob nodded gratefully.

'I'll read it if you like,' TJ said, and Mr Wood handed him the notebook. 'Runners-up in the Inter Schools League,' TJ read. He saw that Rob had made a league table just like the ones in the papers, in very tiny black writing. 'They won nine, drew three and lost none,' he said. 'They scored twenty-five goals and let in twelve. I suppose that means they're very good.'

Rob nodded.

'Their PE teacher reckons they'll win the league this year,' Mr Wood said. 'She's called Mrs Singh and she obviously thinks Hillside School is the best school in town. She didn't actually say so, but I got the impression that she thought Parkview School was the worst school she'd ever come across. She didn't like the teachers, or the mums and dads, or the kids.'

There were loud mutterings from around the classroom, and for once Mr Wood didn't order them to be quiet.

'I know,' he continued. 'I told her she was wrong. I told her you were good kids and this was a good school, and I told her you're just as good at football as they are. So we're going to take them on, in three weeks' time, right here on our own pitch.'

'But, Mr Wood,' said Tulsi, 'we haven't *got* a pitch.'

CHAPTER 10

'I'm going to talk to Mr Burrows this morning,' Mr Wood said. 'I'm sure when he hears about this he'll want to get the pitch repaired. And I'm going to ask him to buy us a proper kit too. All you have to do is train hard and do what I say. Don't look so scared!'

'But we know them, Mr Wood,' Tulsi said. 'We see them in the park. They're much better than us. That Krissy Barton plays in the Sunday League. She's brilliant.'

'Now you listen to me,' Mr Wood said. 'I've coached a lot of teams and I've played in a lot of football matches. There's nothing you can't do if you work together. Just imagine how you'll feel when you beat them!'

TJ tried to imagine it, but he couldn't. He remembered how the three kids in the park had played, rattling the ball around like a pinball machine. It was impossible to think Parkview could beat them. When they went outside at break time, TJ could see that the others agreed with him. They stood on the edge of the playground, looking at the pitch.

'I can't imagine anyone playing on that ever again,' Tulsi said.

'It's just as well,' agreed Rafi. 'We'd never beat that lot in a million years.'

'I don't know why you're saying that,' Rob said.

'What do *you* want?' demanded Tulsi. 'Why do you keep following us around?'

'You're just being mean to him because

he told you you don't run,' Jamie said. 'But he's right about that. You can't argue with the stats. What do you mean, Rob?'

'Football is a simple game,' Rob said. 'With a coach as good as Mr Wood there's no reason why you can't beat them, as long as you do the simple things properly. You know – pass, control, move, shoot. And play like a team. Mr Wood goes on about it enough. But you don't actually *know* if you'll be good or not. Not yet. So you might as well try.'

'Well, we still haven't got a pitch,' sniffed Tulsi.

And when Mr Wood came back into the classroom after break, it looked as if Tulsi was right after all. Mr Burrows followed Mr Wood into the room.

'Mr Wood has just been to see me,' he said, 'and I've come to give you the bad news myself. I'm afraid there's not the slightest chance of getting the playing field mended. We simply don't have the money. So we can't go buying football kit either. I'm very sorry.'

The door swung closed behind him. There was a long silence, then Mr Wood said, 'I'm sorry too. I really thought . . . Yes, TJ, what is it?'

'Mr Wood, couldn't we fix the pitch ourselves? I could borrow some tools from home. We could come to school at the weekend. If we all worked all day, then maybe we could do it.'

Nobody said anything for a moment and then, suddenly, everyone was talking at once.

'My dad's got a spade.'

'I could bring my grandad's garden roller.'

'It can't be that difficult.'

'Stop!' said Mr Wood, holding his hands in the air. 'Some things would still cost money. We'd need turf to fill those holes and—'

'My mum works in a garden centre,' said a girl with red curly hair. 'I could get her to ask if there's any spare turf.'

TJ looked around the classroom. Suddenly it wasn't just the people who'd been playing football who were interested. It was everyone! All of them had ideas about how to help.

'I bet we could mend the kit too,' Cameron said. 'My dad's really good at putting patches on things.'

Mr Wood laughed. 'OK, then,' he said.

'You've persuaded me. But we'll have to get Mr Burrows to agree. How about you and Jamie coming to see him with me, TJ?'

When they entered the head teacher's office at lunch time Mrs Logan was there too, and Miss Berry. 'Well?' said Mr Burrows. 'What now?'

'Perhaps TJ can explain,' said Mr Wood.

TJ's hands were sweating, and his heart was pounding. He wasn't sure why Mr Wood had chosen him, especially since Mrs Logan had been giving him filthy looks ever since he'd jumped over the garden wall. He took a deep breath and began.

'We thought we could repair the football pitch ourselves,' he said. 'We'd all help. Everyone in Year Six. Maybe some of our mums and dads will help too. We thought we could do it on Saturday. Hayley's mum works in a garden centre and she might be able to get some grass.'

Mrs Logan gave a hollow laugh. 'How many parents came to our last Open Day, Mr Burrows?'

'Six,' said Mr Burrows gloomily.

'Your classmates say they'll help, young man, but you'll find that they won't turn up on the day. They'll be far too busy playing computer games in their bedrooms. And as for their parents . . .'

'Mine will help,' TJ said stubbornly. 'I know they will.'

'Mine too,' said Jamie.

'Mr Coggins would have to open the school,' Mr Burrows said thoughtfully. 'On a Saturday morning. He wouldn't like that.' For some reason, that thought seemed to please Mr Burrows.

'I'll ask him,' Miss Berry interrupted. 'I'm sure Mr C will do it for me. I think it's a marvellous idea.'

'Will he?' said Mr Burrows. 'You amaze me, Miss Berry. Well, in that case I really can't see any reason why you shouldn't go ahead.'

Mrs Logan pursed her lips and looked disapproving.

'Thanks, Mr Burrows,' said TJ and Jamie together.

'Don't blame me if the whole affair is a disaster,' Mrs Logan said as they left the room. 'And it will be, you mark my words.'

CHAPTER 11

'You're really taking this seriously, aren't you, TJ,' his mum said that night, when TJ told her about the plan to repair the pitch.

TJ could only nod, as his mouth was full of spicy chicken.

'Well, we'll all help. Your dad's already been talking to loads of people. He's got this idea about starting a Parents' Association. We might even have some fun.'

'Fun!' said TJ's big sister, Lou. 'It sounds like hard work.'

'Jamie's got a big brother,' TJ said. 'He goes to your school. He's called Matt. He said he'd be there.'

'Oh. Well, I suppose I might come,' Lou said. 'If I have time.'

TJ grinned to himself. Jamie had told him that Matt liked his big sister. It looked as if his big sister liked Matt too! Not that TJ was bothered about that, just as long as they both came along to help. 'Thanks, Mum,' TJ said, jumping up from the table. 'The chicken was great!'

'Where are you going?'

'I have to practise,' TJ said. 'We've got training tomorrow night. I think a lot of people are going to come. I want to make sure I get in the team.'

'What about your homework,' his mum called after him.

'I'll do it later,' TJ called back.

Out in the garden TJ practised catching and diving. He hit the ball against the wall, trying to catch himself out. It didn't take him long to grow bored. And he had to admit, he hadn't really enjoyed being in goal during training either. It occurred to him that, actually, goalies hardly ever had to save penalties, or even shots. Most of the time they just stood around waiting for something to happen. It would be much more interesting to be on the pitch.

He dropped the ball, caught it on his foot and held it there. Then he flicked it up and caught it on the other foot. He'd been practising doing this secretly in his bedroom, and he was getting good. He began to practise keepie-uppies. His record so far was 139, but he was sure he could do a lot more.

He had reached 250 when he heard the door open behind him. He took his eye off the ball for a split second and it dropped to the ground.

'You shouldn't be wasting your time in

goal,' Joey said. 'You're mad.'

'I want to be in the team and no one else wants to do it,' TJ said. He wasn't going to admit to Joey that he was having doubts. 'I need to practise. Come on, take some shots at me.'

TJ saved everything Joey hit at him. 'Can't you shoot harder?' TJ asked him.

'How about I go in goal and you show me how,' said Joey.

TJ laughed. 'OK,' he said. He placed the ball carefully, took four steps back, then ran up and hit it. It slammed into the wall before Joey could move and rebounded into the garden fence. Joey looked worried.

'You want to be careful doing that,' he said. 'What if it had hit me?'

'It wasn't that hard, was it?' TJ said, looking down at his foot.

Joey shook his head. 'You are something, you know that? You don't know your own strength. Oh, and Dad sent me out to tell you to do your homework.'

TJ followed him inside, wondering. He wasn't really all that strong, was he?

The following afternoon, almost everyone in Year Six stayed behind after school for training. Lots of mums and dads stayed to watch too, and to TJ's surprise Miss Berry showed up in a tracksuit. They all jogged around the playground and then Mr Wood put them through lots of exercises – sprinting and turning, dribbling with both feet, passing and controlling. When TJ paused for a moment to catch his breath he

saw that absolutely everyone was working.
Rob was sitting on a bench, as usual, but as
TJ watched he saw Mr Wood jog over to him
and ask a question. It was almost as if
Mr Wood was asking Rob's advice. Then
Mr Wood blew his whistle and called them
all together.

'We don't have a lot of time before the big
match,' he said, raising his voice so that all
the spectators could hear. 'And I hope all
you mums and dads will come along on
Saturday to help us get the pitch ready.
Maybe there's someone who'd like to lay
on refreshments?'

'I'll organize that,' said TJ's dad. 'Don't you worry.'

Mr Wood turned to the waiting players.

'We're going to have two matches now, seven-a-side. I've marked out the pitches with cones. Reds v Blues here, and Greens v Yellows over there with Miss Berry. I'll be watching all of you. Everyone here has the chance to be in the team. All you have to do is play well. This is your chance to show us what you can do.'

CHAPTER 12

TJ pulled on a blue bib. Danny, Jamie, Rafi, Rodrigo, Tulsi and Tommy were all in his team.

'Don't just stand in front of the goal this time,' Danny said to Tulsi.

'Shut up, Danny,' Jamie said. 'You can't talk. You just kick people.'

'At least I know which *way* I'm kicking,' Danny replied. 'Not like Rafi.'

'Hey,' said Tommy. 'It's only a game. You OK, Rodrigo?'

Rodrigo grinned. 'Football good,' he said.

TJ pulled on the goalkeeping gloves his dad had given him that morning. If they kept on arguing like this, he thought, probably none of them would get in the team.

'Right,' said Mr Wood. 'I'm in charge of this game, and Miss Berry will look after that lot over there. We've got special rules today, just to keep you on your toes. You're only allowed three touches – two to get the ball under control, and one to pass or shoot.'

Mr Wood demonstrated carefully so that Rodrigo would understand. Rodrigo nodded, but there was a chorus of protest from the others.

'We'll never be able to do that,' Rafi said.

'Try it and see,' replied Mr Wood. 'You might surprise yourself, Rafi.'

He blew his whistle and Tulsi tapped the ball to Tommy. He stopped the ball – and instantly he was surrounded. Every player on the pitch ran towards him, the Blues all yelling for him to pass to them.

'I can't,' he yelled. 'There's no room.'

'Use the space, Blues,' Mr Wood said. 'Look, you've got a whole pitch to play in.'

Finally Tommy spotted a gap and cleared the ball. They all ran after it except Tulsi. She jogged over and took up her usual position on the edge of the opposition penalty area. Suddenly TJ saw Rafi emerge from the little gaggle of players with the ball at his feet. He took one touch, then another, then another . . .

Mr Wood's whistle blew.

Rafi put his head in his hands. 'I told you,' he said. 'I knew it was impossible.'

Mr Wood sighed. 'Listen,' he told them, 'if you all chase after the ball then none of you have anyone to pass to, do you?'

'What, so you mean we just have to stand in one place, like Tulsi?' Danny said nastily.

'That's not it at all, Danny, although at least Tulsi is thinking. At least she's realized you can't all run around together. No, you all have to look for space. You have to give the person with the ball someone to pass to. But you can't just stand still because then the other team can mark you easily, can't they? Let's try again. Reds, it's your free kick.'

Cameron kicked the ball aimlessly forward and Rodrigo intercepted it easily and controlled it with his chest.

'Good!' called Mr Wood. 'Now move for him, Blues. Give him some options.'

The Blues ran. They ran like mad chickens, first one way, then another.

Rafi raced from one side of the pitch to the other . . .

Tommy sprinted down the wing . . .

Danny darted to the left and collided with Jamie . . .

Jamie just stopped, but Danny bounced off him, stumbled, and collapsed to the ground . . .

Rafi tripped over Danny, rolled three times and lay flat on his back.

Rodrigo was still standing there, with the ball at his feet. He looked confused, and TJ didn't blame him. A lot of the watching mums and dads were bent double, laughing.

The Blue team were a total mess.

'Play on,' said Mr Wood. 'There was no foul.'

Ariyan nicked the ball from Rodrigo's feet. He took one touch and then passed it to Jay. The Red team weren't very good, but they didn't need to be good because Danny was still sitting on the ground, and Jamie was gasping for breath. Jay passed to Cameron.

'Go on, shoot!' he yelled.

The Red goalkeeper was laughing and talking to the kids who were watching behind the goal. Cameron hit his shot and TJ watched the ball coming towards him. An idea blossomed in his head. The ball was at a perfect height and he didn't even try to catch it with his hands. Instead, he drew back his foot and struck a perfect volley.

At the last moment, just as he made contact, he remembered Rob's words of advice and kept his knee right over the ball. It flew straight and true, whistling past Jamie's ear, flashing past Tulsi's astonished eyes. It didn't seem to have lost any speed at all as it blasted right through the centre of the Red goal.

If there had been a net, it would have

bulged. Maybe it would even have burst! But there wasn't a net, and so the ball carried on, past the stunned spectators, past the big red nose of Mr Coggins, and straight into the stomach of Mr Burrows, who had just emerged from the school. He staggered backwards into the doorway. Mrs Logan rushed to his side and helped him back onto his feet. He brushed her aside and marched down the steps, very red in the face, clutching the ball in both hands.

'This is ridiculous!' he said. 'It is obviously far too dangerous. Imagine if I had been an elderly lady or a little child! That's it, I'm afraid, everybody. We'll have no more football. You can call off this match. I really can't see what's wrong with rounders. Far more sensible, if you ask me.'

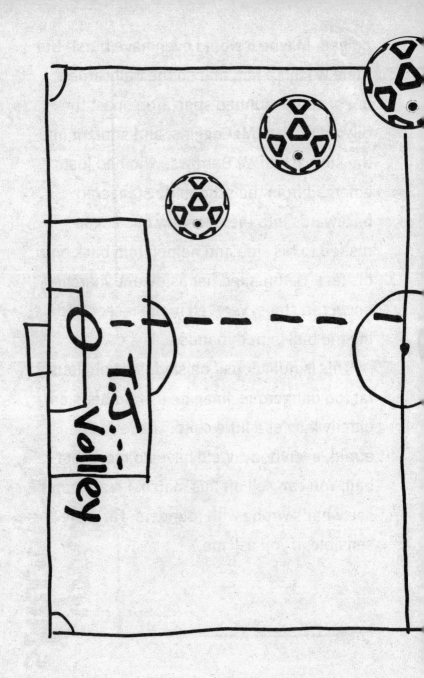

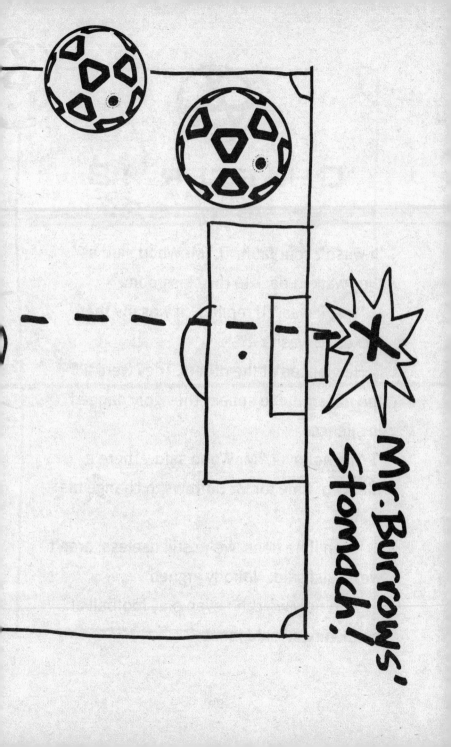

Mr. Burrows' Stomach!

CHAPTER 13

'It wasn't your fault, TJ,' Mr Wood said as they walked back to the classroom.

'Yes, it was,' TJ replied. 'It was me that kicked it, wasn't it?'

He glanced at the others. They were all too miserable to speak. They got changed in silence.

'It's not over,' Mr Wood said. 'There's plenty of time for Mr Burrows to change his mind.'

'Even if he does, we're still useless, aren't we?' Tulsi said. Nobody argued.

'And now we can't even play football at break times,' said Jamie.

'I promise you,' Mr Wood told them, 'I'll get him to change his mind. And you shouldn't give up before you've even begun.'

TJ's mum and dad were waiting for him outside the gate. 'Who's your friend?' his dad asked, looking at Rob.

'This is Rob. I told you about him. He does the stats.'

'Oh, right,' said TJ's mum. 'I don't suppose there was much you could write down about that match, though.'

'Well, actually there was,' Rob said. 'TJ's volley travelled nearly twenty-five metres without touching the ground. It's a very difficult skill, volleying the ball, you know.'

TJ's dad laughed. 'Even more difficult to hit a head teacher at that distance, I should think. Has it ever happened before, Rob?'

'I don't know,' Rob replied seriously. 'I'll have to look it up when I get home.'

'It's not funny, Dad,' TJ said. 'You heard him. Mr Burrows banned football.'

'You hit that ball hard, TJ. I was impressed. It was just bad luck that it hit the head teacher. And there are other places you can play football. Maybe if we tried again we'd be able to get you into Hillside.'

'Dad! I've got all my friends here.' The words tumbled out of TJ's mouth. 'I know we're not much good, but Mr Wood says he can coach us and I believe him. And anyway, he says Mr Burrows will change his mind.'

'I was joking, TJ,' Mr Wilson said, smiling. 'If Mr Burrows doesn't change his mind, he'll have a lot of mums and dads banging on his door wanting to know why!'

When school finished the following day, TJ persuaded the others to go to the park. Mr Wood had been strangely cheerful all day.

'He's got a plan,' TJ said. 'So we'd better

be ready, hadn't we? We know what we have to do to get better.'

'Oh, what,' said Tulsi, 'so you're in charge now, are you? You got us in this mess in the first place. Why couldn't you just catch the ball like a normal goalie?'

'TJ's right,' said Rafi. 'We never had enough time to practise. Come on, Tulsi, give it a try.'

They tried to play the way Mr Wood had told them, controlling the ball and passing and moving around. TJ was just starting to enjoy himself when he heard a shout and saw the Hillside kids racing into the park on their bikes.

'When Mrs Singh told us about the match we knew it couldn't be true,' jeered Krissy. 'We knew you'd never play us. We heard you haven't even got a pitch.'

'Not yet,' said Rafi defiantly. 'But we will have.'

'So why did you call the match off, then? You're just scared, that's all.'

They didn't wait for a reply but rode off laughing. TJ heard one of them say 'useless' and there was another burst of laughter. Somehow, none of them felt like playing football after that.

They were in the playground on Monday morning when the car arrived. 'What *is* it?' said Rafi, as they gazed in awe at the low-slung red vehicle that had just pulled into the teachers' car park. 'Is it a racing car?'

'It's a Ferrari F430 Spider,' said Rob. 'Top speed, 196 miles per hour.'

'It doesn't look like a teacher's car,' said Tulsi, and then she gasped as they saw a tall black man climb out of the driver's seat.

'What?' said TJ.

'Don't you know who that is?' gasped

Tulsi. 'It's Marshall Jones. He plays for Wanderers. What's he doing here?'

Marshall Jones looked lost. Then he saw them watching him, and he walked through the gate towards them. TJ thought that maybe Tulsi was going to faint. It looked like her legs had gone wobbly.

'Hey!' Marshall said, flashing them a gleaming smile. 'I'm looking for Johnny Wood. Is this the right place?'

'You mean *Mr* Wood?' asked TJ.

'I guess. He's a tall guy. Wears a blue baseball hat.'

'That's him. But what . . . ?'

'Can you find him for me?'

TJ nodded and ran off to fetch Mr Wood. He didn't have to run far, because Mr Wood was already walking towards them across the playground, smiling broadly.

'Hey, Marshall,' Mr Wood said, hugging him. 'I see you've already met the kids I was telling you about. Now you'd better come and meet my boss. He's called Burrows.' He led Marshall off towards the office, but as he went he turned and winked at them over his shoulder.

'I'm in shock,' said Tulsi. 'Am I dreaming? Tell me that really happened.'

'It happened, all right,' said Jamie. 'But I don't know what it means.'

Then Rodrigo surprised them all. 'Marshall Jones,' he said. 'Wanderers. Striker. Very good. I like.'

'Hey, Rodrigo!' Rafi said. 'You're speaking English!'

'He's speaking football, you mean,' laughed TJ. 'But that should be good enough for us.'

At the end of break they were all called into assembly. 'We have a very special visitor today,' Mr Burrows announced. TJ noticed that the head teacher had combed his hair and Mrs Logan had put on a lot of extra make-up. 'Let me introduce Mr Jones.'

Most of the kids in the hall muttered: 'Who?' But when they saw Marshall they gradually realized who he was and everyone began to clap – even the little ones in Reception who just liked making a noise.

'I see that you all, er . . . know . . . er . . . Mr Jones,' Mr Burrows said. He was looking very uncomfortable. 'He has very kindly offered to come back to our school next week and talk to your classes about the life of a . . . er . . . footballer. Is that right, Mr Jones?'

'I'll be very happy to do that. But call me Marshall, please. And I was thinking, maybe I could give the children a little help with their football skills?'

The hall went silent. Mr Burrows turned red. He looked at Mrs Logan, but she was smiling a sickly smile at Marshall.

'Oh, er, but of course,' Mr Burrows said in a strangled voice. 'Thank you very much.'

'And your school team?' enquired Marshall. 'You have a school team?'

Mr Burrows gulped. Mr Wood was trying not to smile.

'School team,' Mr Burrows stammered. 'Yes . . . yes . . . of course we do.'

Mr Burrows sank back into his chair, exhausted, as the whole school applauded Marshall Jones.

CHAPTER 14

It was Saturday morning. TJ and Joey were
waiting outside the school gates when a
car pulled up and Miss Berry climbed out,
smiling.

Mr Coggins heaved himself out of the
passenger seat. 'It's not in my job
description, this isn't,' he grumbled,
looking up at the grey sky and the drizzle
that was falling from it.

'It's *so* kind of you, Mr Coggins,' Miss
Berry said, smiling sweetly at him and taking
his arm. 'I really don't know how the school
would run without you.'

'A whole lot better, probably,' Jamie whispered in TJ's ear. 'Is this it then? There's not many of us.'

It was true. Tulsi had arrived, and Rafi and Rob. Rodrigo stood nearby with his mum and dad. Then there was Joey and Miss Berry and Mr Wood, but that was it.

'My mum and dad *are* coming,' TJ told Jamie. 'But they were still in bed when me and Joey left.'

'My brother Matt's coming too,' Jamie grinned. 'And he'll be fed up if your sister doesn't turn up.'

They all walked across the playground and stood gazing at the field. It was a horrible mess, and suddenly it looked terribly big.

'OK,' Mr Wood said. 'The first thing to do is to fill in that hole that used to be a pond. Just wait here a moment.'

He went out to the street and a few

moments later drove in through the gates and straight across the playground. He opened the back of his car and took out two wheelbarrows and an armful of spades.

'That'll be where the centre circle is,' TJ said, looking at the hole.

'It's a very *big* hole,' said Tulsi doubtfully.

'And a very big pile of earth to put in it,' Rafi said, staring at the heap behind the empty pond. It was covered with straggling weeds and bits of rock and rotting logs.

'They made the hole with a digger,' Jamie said. 'This was meant to be a wildlife mini-hill. The logs and rocks are homes for insects and stuff.'

'Habitats,' said Rob. 'We'd better move them to the edge carefully.'

Mr Wood and Miss Berry heaved the black plastic liner out of the hole and handed out spades and gloves. Rob and Jamie moved the logs and rocks. There was nothing under them but a few woodlice. Then they all started to dig. They worked hard for half an hour and then TJ stopped and straightened up. His back hurt and he was sweating. 'It's hard, isn't it?' said Joey.

'Right,' TJ replied. 'And look. We've hardly done anything.'

'Why did Burrows have to make such an enormous pond?' groaned Tulsi.

'OK, everyone,' Mr Wood said. 'Take a break. It's going to take a long time, this. I was hoping more people would come, but we'll do it on our own if we have to.'

TJ could see that no one believed it. Every time he looked at the hole it seemed bigger, and then there were all the other holes where weeds and brambles had tangled among the dead trees. They would never do it on their own.

Then he heard a clattering on the playground and saw Tommy's red hair zooming towards him on a skateboard, and Tommy wasn't alone. He slid elegantly to a halt and flipped the board up into his hands. 'I brought some mates,' he said with a grin. 'They all want to help.'

There were at least ten of them, teenagers mostly, but some of them were even older.

One of them was nearly as tall as Mr Wood. They all parked their boards and grabbed spades. Other people were arriving too, kids from their class, and their mums and dads, and they'd all brought garden tools. But there was still no sign of TJ's mum and dad.

Then TJ saw their car edging slowly in through the gate. He put his spade down and ran across the playground. 'You're late!' he said. 'I thought you were never coming.'

TJ's dad just smiled and opened the back of the car. He pulled out boxes of drink and cakes and biscuits. 'It's a big job, this,' he said. 'You're going to need refuelling. This lot will get you through the morning. Tulsi's mum and dad are bringing their barbecue. Look, here they are!'

More people were arriving all the time now. 'Your dad's been on the phone all week,' his mum said. 'Everyone's dead keen to help. Look, here's a whole crowd of them.'

Janice and her team of dinner ladies had arrived, and TJ was amazed to see the Reception class teacher following them though the gate. 'It's about time something like this happened,' she said to Janice as they went by. 'That Mr Wood has really stirred things up. This was a jolly good school when I first came here. And I don't see why it shouldn't be a good school again.'

'Exactly,' TJ's dad said. 'People power, that's what we've got here. Who knows what we could do next. Paint some of those windows, maybe? Smarten the place up a bit. We could—'

'We need to fill in these holes before we do anything else, Dad,' TJ interrupted. 'Are you going to help, or are you just going to stand there talking?'

'You've got a nerve,' laughed his dad. 'OK, son, give me a spade and I'll show you how it's done.'

CHAPTER 15

They worked hard all morning. So hard that
TJ never even noticed the tall man in the
woolly hat who wheeled barrow after barrow
full of weeds and dead plants and rubbish
to a heap near the fence. Then he saw that a
couple of the mums were nudging each
other and giggling. 'It's him,' one of them
was saying. 'I know it is.'

'You talk to him, then.'

'I can't!'

Mr Wood put down his spade with a grin.

'Hey, Marshall,' he called. 'There's a
couple of ladies would like to meet you!'

TJ thought he had never seen anyone turn red so fast. But Marshall asked the mums all about their children and the school, and soon they were chatting happily to him while all the other parents and helpers gathered round. When Marshall had finished signing autographs he sat down next to TJ. 'Great food,' he said.

'Mmmmm,' was all TJ could reply with his mouth full of burger.

'Looks like you're going to have a pitch then,' Marshall said. 'Hey, there, nice to meet you.' TJ looked up and saw Tulsi standing there. 'I saw you the other day, didn't I? On the playground?' Marshall said.

Tulsi couldn't speak as Marshall held out a hand. Finally she shook hands with him, but she still didn't say a word. 'You must be Tulsi,' Marshall said. 'Johnny told me about you. Says you've got talent. He says you're going to have a great team.'

'I don't know why he thinks that,' said Rafi, who had joined them. 'Last time we played we were rubbish.'

'Oh, yes,' laughed Marshall. 'Your goalie knocked down the head teacher from twenty-five metres. Always good to have a goalie with a powerful kick!' TJ felt himself going red. 'Anyway,' Marshall said, 'I have a surprise for you guys. But I'll let Johnny tell you once we've finished laying that grass down.'

They looked where Marshall was pointing and saw a truck pulling onto the field with a load of turf on the back. 'Glad to help,' said the man from the garden centre when Mr Wood thanked him. 'Come on, I'll show you how to lay it properly. Football pitch, is it? Better make sure we do it right then.'

By the end of the afternoon the work was finished – and everyone was exhausted. The grey clouds cleared and the sun came out.

The pitch looked a little odd with the big new patches of dark green turf.

'It's not perfect,' said Mr Wood, 'but it's good enough to play football on. Anyone fancy a game?' His question was met with loud groans. 'I didn't think so,' Mr Wood laughed. 'Thanks, everyone, for working so hard. It's been a brilliant day. And I've got some good news for you. Marshall has arranged for ten of you kids to go and watch Wanderers tomorrow. I've put your names in my hat and the first ten to come out will be the lucky ones.'

TJ could hardly bear to watch. Tulsi was the first of his friends to be chosen, then Rafi, Tommy and Jamie. Then two more girls he hardly knew, Leila and Ebony, who screamed when they were chosen. Then Rodrigo and Jay. And then, finally, TJ heard his own name called. Danny's was the last name out of the hat.

'Thank goodness for that,' said his mum. 'You can let go of my hand now, TJ. I thought you were going to crush it to pieces!'

'I'm sorry I can't take everyone,' said Marshall. 'But you can all come and watch Parkview play Hillside. It'll probably be even better than watching Wanderers!'

'Bad luck, Rob,' said TJ, seeing the disappointment on Rob's face.

'It's OK,' Rob said. 'It's on TV. I'll see if I can spot you.'

The next day TJ felt stiff all over. 'You're not the only one,' his mum said when he hobbled downstairs for breakfast. 'I could hardly move this morning.'

'Me neither,' Lou said, but she looked happy enough. TJ had seen her working alongside Jamie's brother all day.

'Is Matt your boyfriend now?' he asked innocently, and enjoyed watching Lou blush.

At lunch time TJ and his dad set out for the Wanderers ground. On the way they picked up Tulsi, Jamie and Rafi. 'I can't believe this is happening,' Tulsi said, for the five hundredth time, as they left the car park in the city centre and mingled with the thousands of Wanderers fans who were making their way to the ground. They reached the end of the street and the Piper Stadium towered in front of them, a glittering wall of glass and steel.

'Over there,' said TJ, consulting the map that Mr Wood had given him. 'We have to find the entrance to the River Lounge.'

They didn't have to search far because Rafi spotted Tommy's red hair and they made their way over to meet him. Tommy's dad had brought Danny, Rodrigo, Leila and Ebony. A few moments later Mr Wood arrived, and TJ was amazed to see that Rob was with him, clutching his notebook in one hand.

'I couldn't leave Rob behind,' Mr Wood told them. 'He's part of our coaching staff. Marshall says he can squeeze him in.' Just then, Marshall appeared in the doorway dressed in a very smart suit and a bright orange shirt.

'We'll meet you kids back here after the game, then,' said TJ's dad.

'Are you crazy?' Marshall said. 'I got seats for all of you! Come on in.'

'You're not playing then?' asked Tulsi, as Marshall led them through an underground passage.

'I've been injured,' Marshall said. 'That's why I had the time to come and help you all.'

'You don't *look* injured,' Rafi said.

'Well, no. I can walk just fine. Run, even. But we're talking about playing in a Premier League match here. They won't let me play until they're absolutely sure my ankle's OK. '

There was a sudden surge of noise from

ahead of them and they emerged from the tunnel into dazzling sunlight. Below them, on the brilliant green pitch, the Wanderers players were going through their warm-ups, almost close enough to touch. Away to their left, the City players were doing the same thing. As TJ watched, they all ran to the side of the pitch and that end of the ground erupted into singing and chanting. 'They always bring a lot of supporters,' Marshall said, as he signed autographs for the fans on either side of them. 'But ours are better,' he added, as the whole stadium echoed to the sound of the Wanderers anthem.

Marshall guided them to their seats, pausing as he went to shake hands with dozens of fans.

'They love Marshall,' Mr Wood told TJ and his friends. 'This is the only club he's ever played for. He's been here since he was sixteen.'

'Mr Wood,' asked TJ. 'How do you know Marshall?'

It was the question they'd all been wanting to ask. But if Mr Wood replied they didn't hear him. In a deafening roar, City kicked off.

CHAPTER 16

Right from the start it all went wrong for Wanderers. Every time one of their players received the ball, a City player was right on top of them, preventing them from passing, forcing them back. City had a small midfield player with spiky blond hair who was completely ruthless in the tackle.

'Gary Devlin,' Marshall said grimly as Devlin slid in to make yet another tackle and come away with the ball. 'He's a complete pain. We have to do something about him.'

But Devlin played a neat one-two with another City player and suddenly he was in the penalty area, driving towards the goal. A tall Wanderers central defender stretched out a leg as Marshall and Mr Wood both leaped to their feet yelling 'NO!' The defender missed the ball completely and Devlin went crashing to the ground. The referee blew his whistle and pointed to the penalty spot. The Wanderers players didn't argue.

The ground fell silent as Chester Smith, the veteran City striker, stepped up to take the penalty. He gave the goalkeeper no chance, planting the ball firmly into the bottom corner, beyond the keeper's outstretched fingers.

City were completely in charge. TJ watched with admiration as their players sprayed passes all around the pitch and the Wanderers players struggled to get hold of the ball.

When the teams left the field at the end of

the first half, the City players applauded their fans, but the Wanderers players shook their heads and looked at the ground.

'I wish I was playing,' Marshall said. 'I *hate* sitting up here, not being able to change anything.'

'Why is Paco Sanchez playing out wide?' asked Rob, looking up from his notebook. 'It's not his best position. He's only touched the ball six times, but all his passes have been good.'

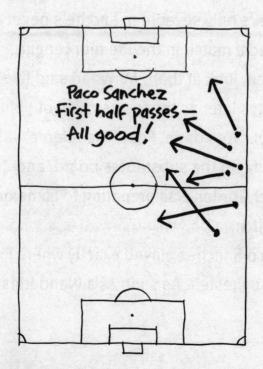

Paco Sanchez
First half passes —
All good!

'You're right,' Marshall said, looking curiously at Rob. 'Paco hates playing out there. That's where I should be, and Paco should be in the centre, just behind the strikers.'

'Well,' said Rob, 'if I was the manager, I'd bring Dexter Gordon on to play wide. He's been doing brilliantly in the reserves. And I'd put Paco back where he should be.'

Marshall shook his head. 'He won't do that,' he said. 'Not in a big game like this. Dexter's only seventeen and he's never even started a match in the Premier League.'

'Well, look at that!' Mr Wood said five minutes later as the teams came out of the tunnel. 'Well done, Rob!' The referee was holding up the substitutes board, and Dexter Gordon was preparing to come onto the pitch.

Paco Sanchez played exactly where Rob had suggested. As soon as a Wanderers defender won the ball, Sanchez was there, calling for it. Most of the time Gary Devlin was right on his heels, but Sanchez controlled every ball that was played to him so quickly that Devlin simply couldn't tackle him without giving away a free kick. As TJ watched, Sanchez received the ball on the Wanderers left, just twenty metres from where they were sitting. Devlin lunged fiercely to try and win it, but Sanchez pulled the ball away so fast that Devlin's boots crashed into his shin. 'OFF . . . OFF . . . OFF . . .' chanted the angry Wanderers fans.

The referee pulled the red card from his pocket and raised it high in the air. After a few moments, Paco Sanchez climbed stiffly to his feet.

'You show them, Paco,' Marshall yelled, and Paco looked up and waved, then grimaced as he put his weight on his leg. 'He'll be fine,' Marshall said. 'He's a tough little guy.'

Paco soon ran off the effects of his injury, but something strange seemed to have happened. 'It's always hard against ten men,' Mr Wood explained. 'They've all pulled back to defend. They're in the lead, after all.'

There seemed to be no space for the Wanderers forwards. Time after time they launched attacks only to find that there was no way through the packed City defence. Out on the wing, young Dexter Gordon controlled the ball and TJ heard spectators yelling at him. 'Skin him, Dexter.'

'Go on, lad, get forward!'

'Take him on!'

But Dexter played a simple pass infield to Paco Sanchez, who spread the ball wide to the other side of the field. The crowd groaned.

'It's the right thing to do,' Rob insisted. 'Wanderers have to keep the ball and make

City run around and chase it. That's how to make the extra man count.'

Marshall laughed. 'Who is your head coach exactly?' he asked Mr Wood. 'Is it you, or is it Rob?'

'Yes!' screamed Tulsi, nearly bursting TJ's eardrum. 'Go on!'

At last, Dexter had found some space, right in front of them, and he was racing down the line. Sanchez saw his chance and played the ball over the head of the last defender right into Dexter's path.

Dexter hit his cross left-footed, curling away from the goalkeeper, and the centre forward's head smashed the ball into the roof of the net. Dwight Fanshawe didn't waste time on celebrations. He grabbed the ball and raced back to the centre circle, giving a thumbs-up to Dexter Gordon as he ran.

The display on the stand read 90.00. Down below them the fourth official held up a board.

'Three minutes,' said TJ. 'Come on, Wanderers!' he yelled.

The whole crowd was yelling now, urging Wanderers forward, but as the seconds ticked away, attack after attack came to nothing. There was time for just one, final attempt. Dexter Gordon hit a cross into the penalty area and the crowd groaned as the City keeper punched it clear. The ball fell towards the ground – and there was Paco Sanchez, waiting. There was no time for him to control it. TJ could see from the shape of his body what he was going to do.

The whole crowd held its breath. Paco's boot intersected perfectly with the ball, and it rocketed towards the goal. There was a loud crack as it hit the inside of the post, flashed behind the keeper and nestled in the bottom of the net.

Chapter 17

Paco Sanchez's volley kept repeating itself in TJ's brain. That, and the way the crowd had reacted. He could still see Paco standing in front of the massive bank of cheering fans with his hands raised in the air and a huge smile on his face. It must be the greatest feeling in the world, TJ thought. And then he thought – *maybe one day that could be me*. It was the first time he had imagined anything like that. Maybe . . .

'Hey, TJ,' Mr Wood said. 'Listen up! You were miles away!'

They were standing on the field. It was the

final training session before their match against Hillside the following day.

'As I was saying,' Mr Wood continued. 'Wanderers won that match by passing the ball and being patient.'

'And by brilliant skill,' TJ interrupted.

'Sure, TJ,' Mr Wood said. 'But you can't score a spectacular volley if your team doesn't have the ball. Let's make sure we know how to keep the ball once we have it. Passing and moving, that's what I want you to do. Make it easy for whoever has the ball to pass it to you. Think about where the rest of the team are. Be ready to pass to them. OK. Let's do it!'

TJ stood in front of the goal. He knew why he was fed up, but there was nothing he could do. He watched as the team began to play better than he'd ever seen them play before, passing the ball and calling to each other. Even Tulsi ran a few metres to make space for Rodrigo to pass to her, then turned and scored a great goal.

'Not bad,' Rob said. He was standing near TJ as usual. 'We might even have a chance.'

'I suppose,' TJ said, kicking the goalpost that Mr Wood had just finished repairing.

'What's the matter?' Rob asked.

'Nothing.'

TJ kicked the post again, and then he heard Jamie yell. He glanced at the pitch and saw that Jamie had played a back pass. He flung himself across the goal, but he was too late, and the ball skidded past him into the net.

'What were you doing?' demanded Jamie.

'You should have looked to see where I was,' TJ told him crossly.

'You should have been ready. You're the goalkeeper, remember?'

'That's enough,' Mr Wood said. 'Anyone can make a mistake. Just remember to concentrate tomorrow, TJ.'

When training was over Mr Wood called them together. 'OK,' he said. 'This is the team for the match. Tulsi, Tommy, Rodrigo, Rafi, Jamie, Danny and TJ. Subs will be Cameron, Ariyan and Jay. Play like that tomorrow and you'll be a match for anyone. TJ, can you wait behind a minute? I want to talk to you.'

'I'm sorry I messed up,' TJ said as the others walked away, talking excitedly. 'I wasn't concentrating. I'll be better tomorrow.'

'It's not that,' Mr Wood said. 'I've been watching you in training, TJ. You're fast. You have excellent ball control. Your friend, Rob, tells me you have the best record of anyone for passes completed in the training exercises. So I just wondered – are you really sure you want to be a goalie? You didn't look happy today. How about, once this match is out of the way, you have a try on the pitch?'

'You mean it?'

'Absolutely.'

'But . . . someone else would have to go in goal. I mean, you'd have to drop someone.'

'It's always like that, TJ. Even for someone like Marshall. Young Dexter Gordon has taken his place in the team at the moment. But it's good for Wanderers to have two great players fighting to play in the same position. And anyway, for this game you stay in goal, OK? It wouldn't be fair on the others to change it now.'

Rob was waiting for TJ in the street. 'What did Mr Wood say?' he asked.

'It was just about the goalkeeping,' TJ replied, hugging his secret to himself. One day soon, he'd get his chance. 'I messed up today. I won't do that tomorrow.'

'We can win,' Rob said, his eyes shining. 'I'm sure we can. I counted sixty-three successful passes, and the movement was excellent.'

'You're right,' TJ agreed. 'And I'm going home to practise. See you in the morning.'

After school the following day, the Parkview School football team changed into their football kit. Cameron's dad had done a great job of mending it. 'I can hardly see the holes at all,' Jamie said.

'Yeah, but that shirt is a bit tight, isn't it?' Tommy laughed. 'Have you been growing, Jamie?'

'A bit,' said Jamie. 'I can't help it. I have to eat.'

Jamie looked as if his shirt might burst apart at any moment, but there was nothing they could do about that. They ran out onto the field just as the Hillside minibus arrived.

There was nothing old or tatty about the Hillside kit. Their boots clattered on the playground as they walked over to the pitch in gleaming red shirts and green shorts. Their teacher, Mrs Singh, stopped them at the edge of the pitch.

'Is this it?' she said to Mr Wood. 'Are you seriously expecting us to play on this?'

'It may look a bit strange,' Mr Wood said, 'but it's perfectly playable.'

'Looks like it's had chicken pox,' said Krissy.

'Or plague,' replied Kelvin.

'Why do we have to play against them?' Krissy demanded. 'We already know they're rubbish.'

'Well, let's prove it, shall we?' Mrs Singh said. 'Over there, please. Start your warm-ups.'

'Well?' said Mr Wood, walking over to the Parkview team. 'What are you all staring at?'

Mrs Singh had laid out cones on the pitch and the Hillside team were already dribbling balls in and out of them in a well-practised routine. 'They're really good,' gulped Rafi.

'And their kit hasn't got holes in,' said Tulsi, frowning.

'And it fits them,' added Jamie gloomily, as his shirt threatened to split.

TJ pulled on his goalkeeping gloves. He was determined that, whatever else happened, he wasn't going to make a single mistake today. After all, it might be his last ever appearance in goal.

CHAPTER 18

'You can stop feeling sorry for yourselves,'
Mr Wood told them. 'There's nothing special
about that lot. I've watched them play. That
teacher has trained them to play like robots.
You guys, you're much better than you think
you are, and you're definitely better than
they think you are. Besides, you've got your
supporters to think about. Look!'

People were pouring out of the school
and onto the playground. There were mums,
dads, grandparents and just about every
child in the school. All the dinner ladies
were there, waving pink pom-poms in the

air. The school cook was there, and even Mr Coggins, the caretaker. Janice and the dinner ladies started chanting: 'PARKVIEW . . . PARKVIEW.' They'd worked out a whole routine with the pom-poms and the rest of the crowd joined in with the singing. It made TJ feel excited and nervous at the same time.

'They won't mind if you lose,' Mr Wood said. 'They know it's your first match. They just want to see you play good football. They want to be proud of the school, so let's get on with it.'

'Mr Wood?' asked Tulsi. 'Who's going to be ref?'

'Mrs Singh. Rodrigo, you're captain. You toss up. Go on.'

Rodrigo gave Mr Wood a huge grin and jogged over to the centre circle.

'Heads or tails,' demanded Mrs Singh.

'*Sim*,' said Rodrigo, looking confused.

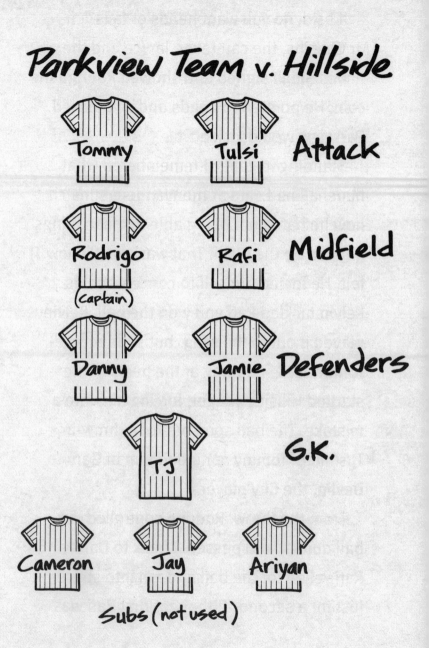

Parkview Team v. Hillside

Tommy — Tulsi — **Attack**

Rodrigo *(captain)* — Rafi — **Midfield**

Danny — Jamie — **Defenders**

TJ — **G.K.**

Cameron — Jay — Ariyan

Subs (not used)

'I said, do you want heads or tails?'

'*Que?*'

Mrs Singh sighed and showed Rodrigo the coin. He pointed to heads and she tossed. Parkview would kick off.

Standing in goal, TJ remembered what Marshall had said at the Wanderers match – how he hated not being able to make things happen on the pitch. That was exactly how TJ felt. He forced himself to concentrate as Kelvin tackled Rafi and won the ball. Kelvin played it out to the wing, but suddenly Tommy was snapping at the heels of the startled Hillside winger, forcing him into a mistake. The ball spun out for a throw-in. TJ smiled. Tommy reminded him of Gary Devlin, the City player.

From the throw, Rodrigo controlled the ball quickly and passed it back to Danny. Rafi yelled for the ball and ran into space. Just for a second, TJ thought that Rafi was

going to start on one of his crazy dribbles,
but instead he spotted Tommy racing down
the wing. It would have been a great pass
if Rafi had kept his eye on the ball.
Instead, he kicked thin air and fell flat
on his back.

As the crowd groaned and Rafi picked
himself up, Krissy was onto the ball in a
flash, running straight at Jamie.

'You can do it, Jamie,' TJ shouted.

Krissy laughed. 'Just you try, fat boy,'
she said and she ran straight past him.
But Jamie was angry. He wasn't going to
let her get away with calling him names.
And anyway, he wasn't fat. He moved fast.
His right leg snaked out and blocked the
ball as solidly as a tree trunk. Krissy went
tumbling to the ground and Jamie cleared
the ball to Rodrigo as the crowd cheered.

Then the whistle blew. 'Foul,' Mrs Singh
pronounced. 'Free kick to Hillside.'

TJ wasn't sure if he should get the others to make a wall, but anyway, it was too late. Krissy smashed the ball towards TJ's goal and he flung himself into the air in a desperate attempt to stop it. He felt something sting his fingertips and heard a crash as the ball thudded into the crossbar, then he was rolling on the ground. He heard Rob's voice yelling, 'Great save, TJ,' and started to pull himself to his feet. Danny got his head to the ball and it flew straight up into the air. Everyone was yelling.

'Clear it, Jamie,' TJ yelled. 'Anywhere!'

Jamie swung his boot. TJ realized, too late, what was going to happen, and he could only stand and watch as the ball cannoned off Jamie's shin, and into the net. Jamie put his head in his hands.

'Idiot!' hissed Danny.

'You shut up,' said Tulsi. 'It wasn't his fault. If you'd been working harder it wouldn't have happened.'

'Come on,' Rafi said, grabbing the ball. 'We can still beat them.'

But by half time even Rafi had stopped believing. TJ had watched two more unstoppable shots fly past him, and even Tommy and Rodrigo had stopped smiling. Mr Wood called them together. 'You started off really well,' he said. 'That was very bad luck, that own goal, and it's wrecked your confidence.'

He glanced up and they saw Mr Burrows and Mrs Logan approaching. 'It's a shame,' Mr Burrows told them. 'You were doing jolly well too. I really thought something good was going to happen for once.'

'Well, you know, Mr Burrows,' Mrs Logan said to him as they walked away again, 'perhaps something good *will* happen. Perhaps we shall get back to basics.

Reading, writing, arithmetic . . .'

'Or perhaps we can beat them,' Mr Wood said, turning back to the team. 'TJ, I'd like you to come out of goal and play up front. Danny, you go in goal and Tommy can be a defender. How about it, everyone?'

CHAPTER 19

There was a chorus of protest, and Danny's voice was loudest of all. 'Why me?' he said. 'I don't even *like* being in goal.'

'TJ's never played except in goal,' Tulsi said doubtfully.

'Yeah,' said Rafi. 'We don't actually know if he's any good.'

But Rodrigo was grinning. 'TJ,' he said. 'Mr Burrows. Bam!' He punched the air in front of him.'

'See?' said Mr Wood. 'Rodrigo understands. TJ knocked over a head teacher from twenty-five metres! We're three–nil down and we have to change something. OK, everyone? OK, TJ?'

TJ nodded. He peeled off the gloves and handed them to Danny.

'Go on, Danny,' Mr Wood said. 'It's for the team.'

'It's for TJ, more like,' grumbled Danny as he pulled the gloves on. 'You'd better be good,' he said to TJ.

They walked out onto the pitch. TJ's legs felt like jelly.

'He's your goalie,' Krissy said to Tulsi. 'Are you desperate, or what?'

'You'll see,' Tulsi said.

'Hey, TJ, you're on the pitch!' TJ looked round and saw his whole family standing on the touchline close by. 'And about time too,' said Joey. 'You show them, little brother!'

TJ didn't *feel* as if he was going to show anyone anything, except, maybe, how bad he was. He watched as Hillside kicked off and the ball zipped around the pitch from player to player. The little bunch of Hillside supporters began to shout *'Olé'* with every pass, and TJ began to think he wasn't even going to touch the ball.

The barrel-shaped Kelvin was raising his foot to shoot when Tommy darted in and stole the ball. Tommy passed to Jamie who took a wild swing at it and watched in amazement as it flew straight to Tulsi. She called out, 'Here, TJ,' and slid a pass towards him.

TJ froze. He had the ball at his feet but he didn't know what to do. He heard shouts from behind him.

'Get rid of it, TJ!'

'Pass it, TJ!'

Then one voice rose above the others. 'Remember Dexter! You know what he did.'

Suddenly TJ's mind was clear. He played the ball back to Rodrigo, wrong-footing the player who was sliding in to tackle him, and he raced away down the touchline. He just had to hope that Rodrigo was watching and knew what to do. Too late, the defender realized where TJ was going and turned to chase him, but TJ was fast. And there was the ball! Rodrigo had spotted his run and chipped it into the space behind the defenders. It bounced once and sat up perfectly for TJ to volley, left-footed, past the goalkeeper.

TJ couldn't believe he had done it. He'd scored! And it had been brilliant! He hardly heard the crowd cheering at first. He turned and there was Rodrigo.

'Bam!' Rodrigo grinned, punching the air with his fist.

'Thanks, Rodrigo,' TJ said. 'Excellent pass!' Then he turned to look at the spectators. All the Parkview supporters were going mad, but TJ just had one thing on his mind. Who had shouted?

T.J.'s first goal

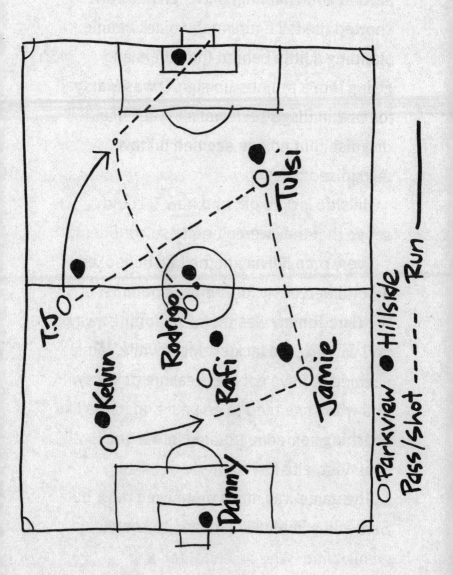

Tulsi

T.J.

Kelvin

Rodrigo

Rafi

Jamie

Danny

○ Parkview ● Hillside Pass/shot —— Run - - - -

The dinner ladies were waving their pom-poms again, and TJ saw his family jumping around and cheering, and then finally he spotted the tall figure in the black beanie, standing a little behind the others and giving him a thumbs-up sign. It was Marshall Jones – in disguise! It wasn't much of a disguise, but no one seemed to have recognized him yet.

Hillside kicked off, and now TJ could sense that they weren't quite so confident.

Every time Kelvin got the ball he looked around nervously for Tommy, and most of the time Tommy was there, scrapping away and winning the tackles. Meanwhile, Jamie seemed to have got the measure of Krissy, and when she tried to go past him it was like watching someone running into a brick wall. TJ almost felt sorry for her.

The game was much more even now, but Slim still somehow managed to keep winning the ball back, no matter how hard Rafi and Rodrigo chased around after him. TJ could see that they needed help. When Jamie made yet another tackle on Krissy and the ball rebounded towards Slim, TJ raced back, controlled the ball on his thigh, hooked it over Slim's head and then nipped round him to touch the ball into Rodrigo's path. Rodrigo gave it back to him, and TJ was away, running at the last defender.

There was no need for tricks. He knew he was faster than the defender so he simply pushed the ball to one side and ran after it. The goalkeeper had come out to the edge of his penalty area, spreading himself as wide as he could. TJ passed the ball, right-footed, between his legs and into the empty net.

The Hillside players were hanging their heads. The big defender TJ had just skinned was bent double, gasping for breath.

'We can do it,' TJ said to Tulsi, as they waited for Hillside to restart the game. 'Look at them! They've had it.'

He realized that Tulsi was staring at him.

'You said you'd never played before,' she accused him.

'I haven't. Only messing around in the garden and that time in the park, kickarounds in the playground. I never played a match in my life.'

'You must have done. No one could—'

'Look out,' yelled Rafi. 'They've kicked off.'

Slim had the ball at his feet, and he definitely hadn't given up. He dodged past Rodrigo and sidestepped a clumsy challenge from Jamie, then unleashed a shot at Danny's goal. Slim was already celebrating when Danny dived full-length and the ball thudded into his body. He stood up holding it and looking a little surprised, but not as surprised as Slim.

'Give it to Tommy,' TJ yelled. Danny's throw found Tommy wide on the wing. He raced down the pitch with the ball at his feet. He was flying towards the dead-ball line, and defenders were sprinting to cut him off.

'Idiot!' said Tulsi. 'He's gone too far.

But TJ knew exactly what Tommy was going to do, and he was already sprinting, flat-out, towards the penalty spot. At the very last moment, just as the ball was about to run out of play, Tommy wrapped his foot around it and produced a perfect cross. TJ flung himself into the air. He kept his eyes wide open and fixed on the ball as he headed it down . . . and into the net.

The scores were level, and TJ had scored a perfect hat-trick – one with his right foot, one with his left foot and one, amazingly, with his head!

'You're a star, TJ!' yelled his sister from the touchline.

'Jolly well done, TJ,' called Mr Burrows. He had taken off his tie and was waving it in the air.

As they jogged back into their own half, Mrs Singh was talking to her team. 'That boy is their key player,' she was saying. 'You have to mark him more tightly. Off you go. I'm expecting you to win, Hillside.'

TJ watched as Krissy said something to Kelvin. They both looked his way, and Kelvin nodded. They obviously had a plan, and TJ didn't have to wait long to find out what the plan was.

The very next time he received the ball, he heard thudding footsteps behind him and suddenly he was flying through the air. He hit the ground with a thump that knocked the wind out of him, and when he stood up his leg didn't seem to be working properly.

CHAPTER 20

'It's a dead leg,' Mr Wood said. 'And it was a very nasty tackle,' he added to Mrs Singh.

'It was clumsy,' Mrs Singh said. 'But I'm sure Kelvin didn't mean to commit a foul.'

'I hope not,' Mr Wood said. 'This is supposed to be a friendly game. How does it feel now, TJ?'

TJ took a couple of steps. His thigh hurt, but it wasn't too bad. 'I'll carry on,' he said. 'But I don't think I can run very far. Or very fast.'

'We can beat them anyway,' Rafi said. 'Even if they do cheat.'

'Are you sure you're OK, TJ?' his mum

called anxiously from the touchline. TJ nodded.

'Don't worry,' said Marshall, who had come to stand beside TJ's dad. 'If Johnny says he's OK, then he is.'

Marshall had taken his hat off and some of the Hillside supporters had recognized him and were waving and pointing from the opposite touchline.

Krissy Barton was staring at Marshall with her mouth open. 'That's Marshall Jones,' she said to Tulsi. 'Has he been helping you?'

'He's Mr Wood's friend, that's all,' Tulsi said. 'And he's one of our supporters,' she added proudly.

'Johnny?' said TJ's dad. 'Johnny Wood? It's been bothering me. I've seen him somewhere before, but I just don't know where.'

'Are you a Wanderers fan?' Marshall asked him. 'Well . . .'

TJ didn't hear the rest because the whistle

blew and the game restarted. Rafi was right. Even without TJ's runs, Parkview began to overpower the Hillside team. The ball flew from player to player so fast that the Hillside players were left chasing shadows. They couldn't get near the ball, and now it was the Parkview supporters who began to chant 'Olé'. But all the passing wasn't getting them any nearer to the Hillside goal because all of the Hillside players had fallen back, blocking the way, determined not to be beaten.

Then Rodrigo passed the ball out to TJ. He hobbled towards it, and touched it forward with his left foot. Out of the corner of his eye he saw Mrs Singh looking at her watch. He had to do something quickly, or it would be all over. And then he saw his chance. Tulsi had pulled away to the right, taking a defender with her, but now she was running in again, towards the goal.

TJ took one more touch. He had to hit it now, but he was going to have to use his left foot. His right leg wasn't much use for anything but standing on. He remembered practising in the garden and he pictured to himself just how he wanted to strike the ball. He used the outside of his foot to make it curl past the defenders – and it was a perfect pass! He held his breath as Tulsi raced forward and blasted the ball into the net.

The crowd went wild. Tulsi turned with her arms high in the air and a huge smile on her face. Then she ran to TJ and whacked him on the back so hard it almost made him forget the pain in his leg.

'That was just brilliant, TJ! It was the best goal I've ever scored.'

The Hillside players looked miserable as they kicked off. They knew there was no time left for them to come back and sure enough,

just seconds later, Mrs Singh blew the whistle for the end of the game.

TJ shook hands with Slim, as the Parkview supporters cheered and the dinner ladies threw their pom-poms into the air. Mr Coggins was doing a crazy dance with Miss Berry and TJ hoped he wouldn't hurt himself.

Slim gave a rueful grin. 'Great hat-trick,' he said. 'But next time, we'll be ready for you.'

TJ's dad ran onto the pitch and clapped him on the back. 'Brilliant,' he said. 'That was even better than watching Wanderers! It was amazing!'

TJ's mum pushed his dad out of the way and gave TJ a big, embarrassing kiss, but he was too excited to care. 'Look!' he said. 'The whole school must be here. Even Mr Burrows looks pleased.'

'So he should,' Tulsi's mum said. 'Lots of people are congratulating him but none of this would have happened without Mr Wood. Why, Mr Burrows wanted to *ban* football a couple of weeks ago.'

'I want to see Mr Wood,' TJ's dad said. 'Where is he?'

'Over there,' TJ said.

On the other side of the pitch, Mr Wood was talking to Mrs Singh and the Hillside team while Marshall chatted to them, and their mums and dads took photos with their phones. Mr Wood waved goodbye and walked back towards them.

'It's a bit sad,' Tulsi said. 'Getting all excited like that just because Marshall is famous.'

TJ stared at her. 'You were exactly the same,' he said.

'No I wasn't.'

'Hey,' said Mr Wood. 'No more arguments! Not after a performance like that. They're a nice bunch,' he said, waving again as the minibus pulled away. 'But they're not used to losing.'

'You used to *play* for Wanderers,' TJ's dad said to him. 'Why didn't you tell us? I knew I'd seen you before.'

'I was just a kid,' Mr Wood said. 'Marshall was my best mate. We weren't much older that this lot here when we first met. And if you saw me play for the first team, you were one of the only ones. I only ever played two games before I got injured and decided to be a teacher.'

'And it's a good job for you lot that he did,' Marshall said, putting an arm around Mr Wood. 'Now you have a football team at last. Not to mention a pitch and a whole load of happy supporters.'

All the people who were standing nearby cheered, and Janice the dinner lady planted a wet kiss on Mr Wood's cheek.

'If only the school wasn't falling to bits,'

said TJ's mum. 'It's a real shame. It doesn't seem fair.'

'We can fix it,' said Rafi's dad, 'just like we fixed the pitch.'

'He's right!'

'It's true!'

'Listen,' Marshall said. 'You know the best thing about today? It was great that TJ came from nowhere and scored a terrific hat-trick . . .' Everyone applauded and TJ felt hot and pleased at the same time. 'And Tulsi's winner was spectacular. But the best thing was the way you played like a real team. Rodrigo was a great captain. He always stayed calm. Tommy and Jamie stopped almost everything in the second half, and when someone did get past, Danny made that fantastic save. And Rafi was everywhere!'

Everyone laughed again when he said that, and suddenly TJ heard Rob's voice.

'I think Rafi ran nearly two kilometres,' he said. 'I can't be exact. There was a lot going on.'

'Ah, Rob,' said Mr Wood. 'Our chief scout and master tactician! Come out here, Rob.'

 Rob emerged from the crowd with his dad. His dad was just like him, small, with glasses and the same curly hair.

'It was Rob who said I should bring TJ out of goal,' Mr Wood said. 'Every great manager needs a great assistant!'

Rob turned bright red.

'Thanks, Rob,' TJ whispered.

'You see what I mean?' continued Marshall. 'You've got a great team here. Look at the work you all did to get this pitch ready to play on. If you can do that together, then I reckon there's nothing you can't do!'

There was an enormous cheer. Even Mr Burrows was clapping, and TJ suddenly realized that he looked a lot younger. He wasn't actually old at all. It was just the lines of worry on his face that made him look that way. Even Mrs Logan seemed a little less scary as she gazed admiringly at Marshall.

Maybe they could make the school better, TJ thought. It was funny how it seemed like a different place already, now that they all had something to celebrate together. And this was just the beginning. Marshall and Mr Wood had been like him once. There must have been a time when they'd played for the first time, maybe on a pitch just like this one. And, for both of them, a day had come when they had run out in front of forty thousand cheering fans to play for Wanderers for the first time . . .

It could be me, he thought.

One day, it could be me.

Rob's stats

Parkview		Hillside
4	Goals scored	3
4	shots	6
4	shots on target	3
38	Passes	37
2	Crosses	3

Goals scored for Parkview

T.J.   3

Tulsi   1